Because of Low

Because of Low

Abbi Glines

SIMON AND SCHUSTER

First published as an eBook exclusive in Great Britain in 2012 by
Simon and Schuster UK Ltd
This paperback edition published in 2013
A CBS COMPANY

First published in the USA in 2012 by Simon Pulse,
an imprint of Simon & Schuster Children's Publishing Division.

Simon & Schuster UK Ltd
1st Floor
222 Gray's Inn Road
London WC1X 8HB

Simon & Schuster Australia, Sydney
Simon & Schuster India, New Delhi

A CIP catalogue record for this book is available from the British Library.

www.simonandschuster.co.uk

E-BOOK ISBN: 978-1-47111-741-1
PBOOK ISBN: 978-1-47113-465-4

Printed and bound by CPI Group (UK) Ltd, Croydon, CR0 4YY

www.simonandschuster.co.uk
www.simonandschuster.com.au

To my best friend, Monica Tucker.
Thank you for listening to all my ideas,
and for always being there, no matter what.

ACKNOWLEDGMENTS

I have to start by thanking Keith, my husband, who tolerated the dirty house, the lack of clean clothes, and my mood swings while I wrote this book (and all my other books).

My three precious kiddos, who ate a lot of corn dogs, pizza, and Frosted Flakes because I was locked away writing. I promise, I cooked them many good hot meals once I finished.

To Monica Tucker, my best friend, and Becky Potts, my mother. They both were my first readers for *Because of Low*. My mother made sure to circle every bad word Cage York said and ask me to change it. I've never laughed so hard. It was priceless.

To Tammara Webber, who is not only my critique partner but my friend. We've taken this wild ride together and I am so very thankful for her advice and level head. She always seems to have it when I need it the most.

To the incredibly amazing team at Simon Pulse—Bethany Buck, Mara Anastas, Anna McKean, Paul Crichton, Lucille Rettino, and Carolyn Swerdloff. Going with a publisher terrified me, but this bunch makes me wonder how I ever did anything without them. They're awesome, and I am so very thankful for them.

To the coolest agent to ever grace the literary world, Jane Dystel. I adore her. It is that simple. And a shout out to Lauren Abramo, my foreign rights agent who is doing an amazing job at getting my books worldwide. She rocks.

And of course I have to mention my FP girls. I'm choosing not to share what "FP" stands for because my mother may read this and it will give her heart failure. Kidding . . . maybe. You girls make me laugh, listen to me vent, and always manage to give me some eye candy to make my day brighter. You are truly my posse.

If I had known who she was when I first met her, would it have made a difference? I honestly can't tell you. The moment Willow Foster entered my life, everything shifted. While my family fell in shambles around me, she remained my core. My center. Then everything she was exploded, twisting into my worst nightmare. I couldn't hold on to them all. I had to choose: Willow or my family. There was no other choice.

Chapter One

MARCUS

Moving back home sucked. Everything about this town reminded me of why the hell I'd wanted to get away. I had a life in Tuscaloosa, and I needed that life to escape. Here, I was Marcus Hardy. No matter where I went, people knew me. They knew my family. And now . . . they were talking about my family. Which is why I had come home. Leaving my sister and mother here to face this alone was impossible. The scandal hovering over our heads took away all my choices and my freedom. Right now few people knew, but it was only a matter of time. Soon the entire coastal town of Sea Breeze, Alabama, would know what my dad was doing—or should I say, who my dad was doing. King of the Mercedes car dealerships along the Gulf Coast had been a high enough title for some little gold-digging whore only a few years older than me to jump into bed with my dear ol' dad. The one time I'd seen the home wrecker working behind the desk right outside Dad's office, I'd known something wasn't right. She was young and smoking hot and apparently money hungry.

Dad couldn't keep it in his pants, and now my mom and sister would have to deal with the stigma it would cause. People would feel sorry for my mom. This was already devastating to her, and she didn't even know yet that the other woman was barely a woman. My younger sister, Amanda, had caught them going at it late one evening when Mom had sent her over to the office to take Dad some dinner. She'd called me that night crying hysterically. I'd withdrawn from school, packed my things, and headed home. There was no other option. My family needed me.

A knock at the door snapped me out of my internal tirade, and I went to see what chick was here looking for Cage this time. God knew the guy had an endless line of females parading through his life. My new roommate was a player. A major player. He put my best friend, Preston, to shame. I twisted the knob and swung the door open without peeking through the hole.

The surprise was on me. I'd been prepared to tell whatever tall, willowy, large-but-obviously-fake-chested female dressed in almost nothing waiting outside the door that Cage was busy with another one very similar to her. Except a very natural, almost curvy redhead stood before me. Red-rimmed eyes and a tear-streaked face gazed up at me. There were no mascara lines running down her face. Her hair wasn't styled, but pulled back in a ponytail. She wore jeans and what appeared to be an authentic Back in Black AC/DC concert T-shirt. No belly button drawing attention to a flat, tanned stomach, and her clothes weren't skintight. Well, maybe the jeans were a little snug, but they hugged her hips nicely. My appreciation of her legs in the slim-fit jeans stopped, however, when I noticed the small beat-up suitcase clutched tightly in her hand.

"Is Cage here?" Her voice sounded broken and musical at the same time. I was having a hard time digesting that this girl was here for Cage. She wasn't anything like he veered toward. Nothing was enhanced. Everything from her thick dark-copper hair to the Chuck Taylors on her feet screamed "not Cage's type." And the fact that she was carrying a suitcase—well, that couldn't be good.

"Uh, um, no."

Her shoulders slumped and another sob escaped her. One small, dainty hand flew up in an attempt to mute the sound of her obvious distress. Her nails were even classy. Not too long, with a smooth, rounded tip and soft pink nail polish.

"I left my cell phone"—she let out a sigh, then continued—"at my sister's. I need to call him. Can I come in?"

Cage was out with a swimsuit model who apparently had a thing for college baseball players. I knew from the way he talked he didn't intend to come up for air much tonight. He'd never answer her call, and I hated to see her get more upset than she already was. A horrible thought crossed my mind: Surely he hadn't gotten this girl pregnant. Couldn't he see how freaking innocent she was?

"Uh, yeah, but I don't know if he'll answer. He's busy . . . tonight."

She shot me a sour smile and nodded, stepping around me.

"I know the kind of busy he is, but he'll talk to me."

She sounded rather confident. I wasn't feeling her confidence myself.

"Do you have a cell I can use?"

I reached into the pocket of my jeans and handed it to her, unable to argue with her further. She had stopped crying and I wanted to keep it that way.

"Thanks. I'll try calling first."

I watched as she walked over to the sofa and dropped her suitcase to the floor with a thunk before sinking dejectedly down onto the worn cushions as if she'd been here a hundred times. Being as I'd only been moved in for two days, I wouldn't know if she had been here before or not. Cage was a friend of a friend who had been looking for a roommate. I'd needed somewhere to live fast and his place was nice. Preston was on the same baseball team as Cage at the local community college. Once Preston heard I needed a place to live, he'd called Cage and hooked me up.

"It's me. I left my phone when I ran. You're not here, but your new roommate let me in. Call me." She sniffed, then hung up. I watched, fascinated, as she proceeded to text him. She really believed the male whore I lived with was going to call her right up as soon as he got her message. I was intrigued and growing more concerned by the minute.

She finished and handed the phone back to me. A smile touched her splotchy red face and two dimples appeared in her cheeks. Damn, that was cute.

"Thanks. Do you mind if I wait a little bit until he calls back?"

I shook my head,."No, not at all. You want a drink?"

She nodded and stood up. "Yes, but I'll get it. My drinks are in the bottom drawer of the fridge behind the Bud Lights."

I frowned and followed her into the kitchen. She opened the fridge and bent down to get her hidden drink. With her bent over digging for her so-called drink, the snug fit of the faded jeans over her ass was hard to miss. It was a perfect heart shape, and although she wasn't very tall, her legs seemed to go on for miles.

"Ah, here it is. Cage needs to run to the store and restock. He must be letting his one-nighters drink my Jarritos."

I couldn't keep guessing. I needed to know who she was exactly. Surely she wasn't one of his girlfriends. Could she be the sister Preston had mentioned dating? I sure as hell hoped not. I was interested, and I hadn't been interested in anyone in a while. Not since the last girl broke my heart. I'd opened my mouth to ask her how she knew Cage when the phone in my pocket started ringing. She walked over to me and held out her hand. The girl really believed it was Cage. I glanced down, but sure enough, my roommate had called back.

She took the phone from my hand.

"Hey.

"She's such a selfish jerk.

"I can't stay there, Cage.

"I didn't mean to leave my phone. I was just upset.

"Yes, your new roommate's a nice guy. He's been very helpful.

"No, don't end your date. Get her out of your system. I'll wait.

"I promise not to go back.

"She is who she is, Cage.

"I just hate her." I could hear the tears in her voice again.

"No, no, really, I'm fine. I just needed to see you."

"Don't. I'll leave.

"Cage—

"*No.*

"Cage.

"Okay, fine."

She held the phone out to me. "He wants to talk to you."

This conversation was nothing like I'd expected. The girl had to be his sister.

"Hey."

"Listen, I need you to make sure Low stays there until I can get home. She's upset and I don't want her leaving. Get her one of her damn Mexican soda thingies out of the fridge. They're behind the Bud Lights in the bottom drawer. I have to hide them from other chicks I have over. All females tend to like those nasty drinks. Turn on the television, distract her, whatever. I'm only ten minutes away, but I'm putting my jeans on as we speak and headed home. Just help her get her mind off things, but *don't* touch her."

"Ah, okay, sure. Is she your sister?"

Cage chuckled into the phone. "Hell no, she ain't my sister. I'd never buy my damn sister drinks and call her back when I'm in the middle of a fucking threesome. Low's the girl I'm gonna marry."

I had no response to that. My eyes found her standing over by the window with her back to me. The long thick copper locks curled on the ends and brushed against the middle of her back. She was absolutely nothing like the girls Cage regularly hooked up with. What did he mean, she was the girl he was going to marry? That made no sense.

"Keep her there, man. I'm on my way."

Then he hung up the phone.

I dropped it on the table and stood there staring at her back. She turned around slowly and studied me a moment, and then a smile broke across her face.

"He told you he was going to marry me, didn't he?" she said laughing softly before taking a drink of the orange soda with what appeared to have Spanish writing on the label.

"Crazy boy. I shouldn't have bothered him, but he's all I've got."

She walked over and sank back down onto the old faded green sofa, pulling her legs up underneath her.

"Don't worry. I'm not leaving. He'd rip apart my sister's house searching for me and scare the bejesus out of her if I left. I've got enough issues where she's concerned. I don't intend to unleash Cage on her."

I slowly made my way over to the only chair in the room and sat down.

"So, you're engaged?" I asked, staring down at her bare ring finger.

With a sad smile she shook her head.

"Not in a million years. Cage has crazy ideas. Just because he says them doesn't make them true."

She raised her eyebrows and took another drink of her soda.

"So you aren't going to marry Cage?" I really would love for her to clarify this because I was incredibly confused and more than a little interested in her. She bit down on her bottom lip and I noticed for the first time how full it was.

"Cage was my 'boy next door' growing up. He's my best friend. I love him dearly and he really is all I have. The only person I can count on. We've never actually been in a relationship before because he knows I won't have sex with him and he needs sex. He's also real wrapped up in the whole idea that a relationship between the two of us before we get married will end badly and he'll lose me. He has this irrational fear of losing me."

Did she know the guy had bagged more than three different girls this week and apparently was having a threesome when she'd called? She was so much better than Cage.

"Wipe that look off your face. I don't need your pity. I know what Cage is like. I know you have probably seen the kind of girls he's attracted to, and I look absolutely nothing like them. I don't live in a fantasy world. I'm very aware." She tilted her head and smiled at me sweetly. "I don't even know your name."

"Marcus Hardy"

"Well, Marcus Hardy, I'm Willow Montgomery, but everyone calls me Low. It's a pleasure to meet you."

"Likewise."

"So, you're a friend of Preston's."

I nodded. "Yes, but don't hold it against me."

She laughed for the first time, and the sudden pleasure from such a simple sound startled me. I liked hearing her laugh.

"I won't. Preston isn't all that bad. He likes to use those

pretty-boy looks of his to get his way, but I'm safe from his attention. Cage would kill him if he decided to bat his baby blues at me."

Was it because of Preston's womanizing or the fact that he was a guy that made Cage protective of Willow? Did he really expect her to wait around until he was ready to settle down and marry her?

"LOW!" Cage's voice rang out as the door to the apartment swung open. His head snapped around and his eyes went straight to Willow.

"God, baby, I was so afraid you'd leave. Come here." This was a side of Cage I'd never seen. Apparently the sweet little redhead got to him in a way no one else could. He pulled her up into his arms, reached down and grabbed the forgotten suitcase, then led her back to his bedroom, whispering to her the entire way. If she hadn't informed me earlier that she refused to have sex with him, I'd have been eaten up with righteous fury at the idea of him touching someone so sweet after having just left the bed of not one but two girls. But instead, I was eaten up with envy because I knew he was going to get to hold her and listen to her musical voice as she spilled out all her problems. He'd be the one to fix them, not me. I'd just met her. Why the hell did that bother me?

Chapter Two

WILLOW

I glanced down at Cage sprawled out on the floor beside me. He'd somehow managed to find a few blankets and a pillow last night when he'd returned from his two a.m. booty call. He reeked of whiskey and sex. I didn't allow him to sleep next to me when he'd been out screwing some nameless chick, crazy boy. I resisted the urge to reach down and brush the long black hair out of his eyes. I needed to leave, and if I woke him up he'd stop me. My sister was expecting me to keep my niece, Larissa, today. I was still furious with her, but Larissa was a baby and she needed me. She couldn't help the fact that her mommy was a selfish brat.

I took the quilt off the bed as I stood up and gently covered Cage's half-naked body. He'd stripped down to his boxers last night in his attempt to get rid of the smells of smoke, whiskey, and cheap women that had permeated his clothing. Didn't matter he still smelled like all those things. The ridiculously chiseled body of his was always a golden brown. His mother had been one hundred percent Indian and it was obvious in his features. The intense blue eyes of his had to be the only thing his dad gave him genetically or otherwise. That was one of the many bonds Cage and I shared: absent fathers.

My suitcase held the only three clean outfits I currently had. My dirty clothes were piled up over in the corner of Cage's room in a plastic laundry basket. I really needed to make time to do the laundry. Grabbing a pair of jeans and a HURRICANES BASEBALL T-shirt Cage had given me from my meager supply of clothing, I dressed quickly and quietly. After I'd brushed my hair, I closed my suitcase and threw my clothing from last night into the dirty clothes basket.

Gently closing the bedroom door behind me so I didn't wake him, I turned and headed for the fridge. I needed some coffee and I wanted to leave some ready for Cage when he woke up. Lord knows he'd need it after his late night.

"I thought you left last night."

I spun around to see Marcus Hardy sitting at the kitchen table with a newspaper and a cup of coffee already in his hands. I really wish he wasn't so dang gorgeous. Marcus Hardy wasn't in my league, or even my atmosphere. How Cage had landed a Hardy for a roommate, I had no idea. Preston must be really tight with Marcus, which seemed odd since Preston had grown up much like Cage and me.

"Um, no, that was Cage who left last night."

Marcus frowned that disapproving frown I'd seen last night again. He really didn't get Cage and me at all. I wasn't sure if he was judging me or Cage, but it annoyed me. Even though he had the prettiest green eyes I'd ever seen on a guy in my life.

"Cage isn't here?"

I shook my head. "No, he's back. He had a, um, call last night and he went out. He got back a few hours ago."

"So he left you here while he went . . . out."

I sighed and reached for a coffee cup.

"Yep."

"I was going to make me some eggs and toast. You want some?"

That hadn't been the response I'd expected. I was sure he was going to beat this thing with Cage and me into the ground. Instead, he was offering to fix me breakfast.

"No thanks. I've got to go keep my niece today." I held up the coffee mug in my hand. "I take mugs full of coffee with me when I leave, but I always bring them back."

Marcus shrugged, "No worries. They aren't mine anyway."

"I know. I bought them for Cage when he got this place."

Marcus stood up, walked over to the fridge, and began

getting eggs and butter out. If I was honest with myself, I really wanted to stand here and watch him cook. Then eat breakfast with him and see if I could make him smile. I felt sure he had a really nice smile. Those green eyes would probably twinkle.

"If you're sure you can't stay. My cooking is pretty damn impressive."

Marcus reached over to open the drawer beside me. The clean soap smell mixed with coffee and something else that reminded me of warm summer days met my nose. I fought the urge to grab his shirt and take a deeper whiff. He'd think I was crazy. I'd always thought the way Cage smelled when he came home from celebrating a victory game was the best smell in the world. But Cage's sweat, beer, and cigarettes couldn't compete with clean Marcus Hardy.

Okay, I needed to go.

"Um, okay, I gotta run. Thanks again, and I'll take you up on breakfast another time. I've got to get to my sister's place before she comes over here with my niece in tow."

Marcus glanced up and a small frown puckered his brow. He seemed concerned. If the guy only knew this was the least of my problems. I wondered what he would think if he knew I actually had nowhere to live. My sister's couch and Cage's bed were the only options I had for now. Somehow I knew he'd want to fix that, and it warmed me. Shaking my head to clear it of my illusions of Marcus, I stepped around him and his yummy goodness then headed for the door.

"You gonna be okay?" he called as my hand touched the handle. A smile tugged at my lips. I was right. He did care. But then, guys like Marcus wanted to save the world.

"Yep," I replied, glancing back over my shoulder to flash him a smile before stepping outside and heading to my reality.

"Where the *hell* have you been? No, wait, don't tell me. You've been in Cage York's bed again. You know you have no right judging me when you go sleeping with that male whore."

I bit the inside of my cheek to keep from screaming. My sister was so uninvolved in my life she didn't have a clue how off track she was. Yes, Cage was probably considered a male whore, but he did pick really hot, sexy females to screw around with. He had pretty high standards. It never ceased to amuse me that people thought I was one of his many conquests. I didn't fit the profile at all. For starters, he kept me around. He never kept a girl around after he slept with her. Second, I wasn't nearly tall enough, I was redheaded, my hips were too big, and my chest was too real. Cage had a thing for fake boobs. Strange but true. Anyway, my sister was the walking persona of the kind of girl Cage went after. Granted, she had red hair too, but hers was naturally curly and she was tall and thin. Red hair looked better on her than it did me. She made red sexy. Me, not so much.

"I'm here now. Just go, and stop cursing and yelling in front of Larissa. It took me an entire week to get her to stop saying s-h-i-t when she dropped things."

If I wasn't so worried about the fact that it might become a permanent word in her vocabulary, I would've found it funny. She would sit in her high chair and drop one Cheerio at a time. Each time one bounced on the cracked linoleum, she'd yell "SHIT!" and clap her hands and do it again. This was all thanks to my lovely sister yelling "Shit!" every time Larissa dropped her food onto the floor. So my niece had decided to make a game of it.

"Whatever, it was funny. I gotta go. Call Janet Hall, the lady with the sponge rollers always in her yellow hair who lives three houses down and ask her if she can watch Larissa tomorrow. You've got class tomorrow, right?"

I nodded. "Yes."

I hated leaving Larissa with the cat lady. She'd come home with several scratches from the thousands of cats in that house last time she stayed there, not to mention the place smelled like cat poo. But I couldn't miss a class or make less than a B in any of my courses or I'd lose my scholarship. I needed that scholarship. Faulkner was a junior college, and that was all the college I would get. Once my scholarship was up, I wouldn't be furthering my education. Unless I could manage a student loan, and considering I didn't even have a home, that seemed unlikely.

"Okay, I'm gone. Don't call my cell while I'm at work. If you have any problems, just figure them out."

And she was gone. No kiss good-bye to Larissa. I hated her for that if nothing else.

My mother had died of cancer when I was twelve, leaving me and my sister alone in the world. Tawny had been eighteen, and she'd taken custody of me, and luckily the house was paid for thanks to Mom's frugal budgeting over the years. The house had been left to Tawny along with the meager amount of money in the bank. She'd gotten her GED instead of finishing her senior year and had managed to get a job to pay the bills. Once I was old enough to work, I'd gotten an after-school job to help out. Then Larissa had come along a little over a year ago and everything got harder. Tawny told me she couldn't support me any longer and I needed to get my own place. I couldn't afford my own place on a waitress's income. So she decided that if I took care of Larissa for her while she worked she'd let me stay a night free of rent in return. Problem was, she didn't need me to keep Larissa every day, and when I didn't keep Larissa, she didn't let me stay the night.

Sounds harsh, but the truth was I was more than positive Larissa's dad came around those nights and she didn't want me to know who he was. If it wasn't for her secret of who Larissa's daddy was, I am pretty sure she'd let me stay. But I got booted for a guy. At first I went to the Methodist church because they have a homeless shelter, but when Cage found out I was going there because Tawny wasn't letting me stay at home anymore he flipped.

Now I go to his place instead. I tried to fight him on it just because of his crazy notion we're going to get married, but I needed him. Even if he was possessive and insane at times, he took care of me. No one else ever did. He liked knowing he had the ability to take care of someone.

When Cage's grandmother passed away, she left him everything she had saved and tucked inside her mattress. Cage had never even met the woman because his mom had run away from home when she was sixteen and never gone back. It had been a surprise when Cage received a check for over two hundred thousand dollars. The first thing Cage did with the money was buy his apartment. He figured it was a good investment and he wanted some security. The rest of the money he put in the bank, and he only draws the interest. He'd been trying to get me to move in with him ever since.

"Lowlow out," Larissa demanded as she banged her small, pudgy fist on the tray of her high chair. Lately she'd gone from calling me Mama to Lowlow. It infuriated Tawny when she called me Mama. I'd had to work on breaking her of that habit.

"Yes, I'll get you out, but first let's wash the banana off your hands."

MARCUS

"When did Low leave?" Cage grumbled as he stepped out of the bedroom an hour after Willow had left. I could smell the whiskey on his breath from across the room. How'd she sleep near that?

"About an hour ago."

He nodded and pulled his cell phone out of his pocket. I tried to appear as if I was focused on the screen of my laptop instead of curious about what he was going to say to her.

"Hey, baby, why'd you leave without waking me?

"Aw come on. You know I'd wake up for you.

"I'm sorry. I shouldn't have left you.

"No, I shouldn't have. I thought you were sleeping.

"I want you to come back here tonight and please take the key. I keep leaving it out for you. I don't like you having to stay with her, and God help me if I find out you're going back to that damn shelter.

"I'll come get you myself if you don't get your ass over here tonight.

"I got a game tonight. You want to come? I promise to leave with you after.

"Okay, fine. But come here. If you need rest so badly before class tomorrow, then get your sexy ass over here and go to bed. I promise not to stink tonight."

Cage chuckled and hung up the phone.

"That girl's gonna drive me nuts, I swear."

I glanced up from my computer screen. Cage was pouring himself a cup of coffee.

"Did she get some coffee before she left?"

"Yeah, she did."

He nodded and leaned back against the counter.

"She look upset or tired?"

She had looked defeated, but I didn't want to tell him that. Not because I was worried about him, but because I didn't think she'd want me to point out that observation.

"She seemed fine."

I thought about the part of his phone conversation where he'd brought up a shelter. My insides cringed at the thought of Willow sleeping at a shelter.

"What did you mean about her going to a shelter?"

Cage cursed and shook his head. "That sister of hers is mean as hell. She's basically kicked Low out. I didn't know about it at first. I found out she was sleeping at a church in town that had some kind of homeless shelter. I was so fucking furious I could've killed her sister with my bare hands."

"Where does she live, then?" I had a feeling I wasn't going to like his answer, but I needed to know.

"On the days she keeps her niece, her sister lets her stay the night. The rest of the time she comes here. I tried to move her into the room you're staying in several times, but she refuses. Says she can't handle my lifestyle full-time. The only reason I didn't press it is because I'd end up losing her. She'd see what a chickenshit I really am and I'd lose her. I can't lose her."

The guy was really screwed up. How did he think he was really in love with Willow if he couldn't even stop screwing every chick with a pair of long legs and fake tits in order to take care of her and keep her safe?

"I see," I replied, even though I didn't.

Cage chuckled and set his coffee cup down. "Naw, I doubt you see at all."

I didn't respond because he was right.

The knock at the door startled me even though I'd been anticipating it for hours.

Ever since Cage had told me to expect Willow around seven tonight, I'd been surprisingly anxious. I'd have Willow to myself. Even though I knew it wasn't wise, I was looking forward to it. She fascinated me. Although, it bothered the hell out of me that her sister had kicked her out again. Even after she'd kept her niece today.

"Hey, Marcus." She smiled up at me as I opened the door wide and stood back so she could step inside.

"Hey, yourself."

"I hope I'm not interrupting your night. You can just ignore me and go about whatever you were doing. I'll even hide out in Cage's room if you prefer privacy or anything."

No way.

"No, uh, I actually need some company. I've been working

on getting my online courses set up. I need a break and an actual conversation." She beamed, and both dimples flashed at me.

"Oh, good! I brought a DVD I rented from the Red Box and some supplies for a homemade pizza." She held up the large canvas shopping tote in her hand. Clenched in her other hand was the handle of the old suitcase. My stomach twisted at the thought of her having to carry her things around with her. And the fact that such a small suitcase held all she owned. My sister's swimsuit collection wouldn't even fit in that thing.

"That sounds perfect."

"How good are you at chopping veggies?"

I pushed up my sleeves and flexed my arm, "I've actually had some pretty good experience."

She laughed, making me feel like I'd just moved a mountain instead of agreeing to chop vegetables for her.

I followed her into the kitchen and enjoyed the view of her backside. Tonight she hadn't covered those incredible legs with jeans. A pair of khaki shorts and a snug red tank top showcased her flawless peaches-and-cream skin. And that hair of hers was hanging down her back, free of its ponytail. The silky waves seemed almost unreal.

"Okay, I know there is a decent knife in one of these drawers because I brought one over a couple weeks ago. You go on a scavenger hunt for it and a cutting board, and I'll get the veggies washed."

I started looking for the knife while attempting to keep the goofy grin off my face.

"How old is your niece?" I was determined to find out more about her tonight. The girl was an enigma. She glanced back over her shoulder and smiled at me.

"She turned one last month."

I opened a drawer to find the missing knife wedged between two Koozies. "Found it."

"Oh, good. Here, start slicing up the mushrooms," she said, nodding toward the mushrooms lying on the towel still damp from her cleaning them.

"Yes, ma'am."

"So, how do you like living with Cage? I mean, you two are absolutely nothing alike, from what I can tell."

What did she mean by that, exactly? Not that I was upset she didn't think I was a player, but she obviously held Cage in some sort of high regard.

"He's a nice guy. Rarely here. It's been easy to find quiet time for my online classes."

"Cage can't stay put long. He needs to be social. He's always been that way. When we were kids, he was always on the go. So many nights he snuck in my window because he'd stayed out too late and his mom had locked him out."

I couldn't comprehend a parent locking their kid out of the house because they'd missed curfew. My parents were always standing at the door pacing, ready to unleash their punishment if I came home late.

"Stop frowning." She chuckled and nudged my side with her elbow. "I can practically see your thoughts. You're friends with Preston, so you know the kind of home life he had. Well, most of the kids in our neighborhood had the same kind."

I forced a smile and focused my attention on the vegetables.

"No, yeah, I mean, I know."

That made absolutely no sense. Willow let out a soft laugh and began mixing the pizza dough. We worked in silence and I tried hard to focus on the vegetables I was supposed to be chopping while she kneaded and rolled the dough. Her arms were slender, but the small muscle that flexed as she pushed and pulled on the dough was literally mesmerizing. What was wrong with me?

"So, did you come home because you were tired of college life, or do you have some other big plans that explain your sudden change in location?"

She wasn't the first person to ask me this question. I'd been nailed with questions from all my friends who knew I loved life in Tuscaloosa. They also knew I had been looking forward to some space from the girl who had gotten under my skin this past summer. However, Willow was the first person I really wanted to tell the truth to, but it was too soon.

"Family stuff brought me home."

I prepared myself for her to press further like Preston had, but she just nodded and reached over to scoop a handful of the mushrooms I'd chopped and began sprinkling them onto the pizza.

"Family sure can screw things up, can't they?" Her defeated tone tugged at me. Pulling her into my arms and promising her that everything would be okay wasn't the best idea since I'd probably freak her out. Instead, I just nodded and reached over to sprinkle onions on the pizza just so my arm could brush against hers.

"That was one of the best pizzas I've ever eaten," I admitted after helping Willow clean up our mess in the kitchen.

"We make a good team," she said, throwing me a grin over her shoulder as she put the DVD into the player.

I sat down in the straight-back chair, leaving the sofa available for her. There was enough room for both of us on it, but I didn't want her to feel uncomfortable with my sitting beside her. Willow turned around and frowned at me.

"I don't bite, Marcus. You can come sit on the comfy old couch with me. That chair is incredibly uncomfortable."

Just the opening I needed. I jumped up and sat down on the end of the couch and stretched my legs out in front of me.

"You don't have to tell me twice. I was just being polite."

Willow chuckled and brought a blanket over to the sofa with her. She didn't sit at the opposite end, which surprised me. Instead, she sat down next to me just far enough away that our bodies didn't touch, and held up the blanket. "Wanna share?"

"Yeah." I wasn't the least bit cold, but an offer to get under a blanket with Willow wasn't something I was going to pass up.

"All right," she announced as she spread the cover out over both of us. "Here we go."

The dark room was illuminated by the television screen. The warmth from Willow's body was so tempting. I wanted to close the distance between us and run my fingers through her hair. From the moment I'd opened the door last night to see her standing there in tears, I'd been dying to see if it was as soft as it looked. As if reading my mind, she scooted over toward me and laid her head on my shoulder.

"I hope you don't mind, but I'm a cuddler when I watch movies."

I almost choked on my words. "Uh, no, I don't mind."

Even though she'd moved closer, I forced my arm to remain on the back of the sofa and not find its way to her hair.

"I didn't even get a romantic comedy. I thought about you when I rented it, and you don't appear to be a romantic comedy type of guy. I went for sci-fi instead."

With her snuggled up against me on the couch, I would watch the damn *Princess Diaries* I'd abhorred since my sister had forced me to watch it over and over when she was little.

"Sci-fi is good," I assured her, knowing I wouldn't be able to focus on anything with the sweet smell that reminded me of honeysuckle wafting up from her hair.

Chapter Three

WILLOW

"Low," Marcus whispered in my ear. I snuggled closer to the sound and breathed deeply. He smelled so good I wanted to curl up inside his clothes.

"Low, you need to wake up," his voice said a little louder. I stretched and opened my eyes. It took a second for my eyes to adjust to the darkness. But the first thing I saw was the very defined six-pack of Marcus Hardy's stomach peeking out from underneath the dark-blue T-shirt he was wearing. My next realization was that my head was in his lap.

"I'm sorry I had to wake you, but it's after two and I figured you might want to get to bed before Cage gets home."

The warm cotton of his shirt was clasped tightly in my fist. I stared at my hand and quickly released the grip I'd had on his shirt. What the heck? Had I been trying to undress him in my sleep? God, I hoped not.

I sat up and a yawn escaped.

"I'm sorry I fell asleep on you," I mumbled, feeling my cheeks grow warm.

He grinned, and his green eyes twinkled with mischief. "Don't be. I don't know when I've enjoyed a night this much."

I ducked my head and bit my lip to keep a silly grin from breaking across my face.

"Me too. Well, except when I fell asleep."

His deep chuckle sent a warmth through me I didn't recognize. It wasn't something I was familiar with, but it was nice. More than nice. It could be addictive.

"You'd better get to bed. You've got that early class," he said softly.

I nodded, then stood up and made my way to Cage's bedroom door. Turning back before I disappeared inside, I called out, "Good night."

"Good night, Low." His deep voice rumbled in the darkness.

"Hey, baby, I'm home and I'm clean. I scrubbed in the shower and used half a bottle of mouthwash," Cage murmured as he crawled into bed beside me. I forced open my sleepy eyes to see the sunrise on the horizon. I nodded and rolled over to get another hour of sleep before I needed to get up.

"I'm sorry I stayed out all night. I didn't mean to," he whispered, reaching out and clasping my hand in his. I didn't allow him to snuggle up to me in bed. It never ended well. He'd get a hard-on and start trying to feel me up. We'd tried a few times and I always ended up frustrated with him and threatening to sleep on the floor. I didn't want things to get heated with us. Cage was my family. He'd never be anything more.

"S'okay," I muttered.

"Did you have a good evening? I saw you made pizza and left me a few slices in the fridge."

I nodded against the pillow.

"Did Marcus eat with you?"

I nodded again.

"He isn't like us, Low. You know that, right?"

I knew what Cage was saying. Marcus was out of my league. He didn't want me thinking there could ever be anything between me and his roommate. I was low-class. Marcus was a rich kid.

"I'm not stupid, Cage."

"No, you're fucking brilliant. And a guy like Marcus would never get just how fucking perfect and brilliant you are. He'd never see past the other stuff."

I wanted to be mad at him, but I knew he was right. If Marcus ever saw what I came from, what I was, he'd never give me the time of day.

"I know," I whispered into the dark.

"I love you, Low."

"I love you, too."

"Then take this," he said as he slipped a key into my hand and closed my fist over it. "I'll be able to relax knowing you have a key. Please take it."

I didn't respond. I wasn't sure what to say. The fact was, I wanted that key. It gave me a warped sense of reassurance that I would be able to see Marcus even more frequently.

Within seconds he was softly snoring in my ear. I lay there staring at the ceiling. Fate wasn't fair. It loved playing cruel jokes on me. Marcus Hardy was its new joke.

I hadn't expected Marcus to be awake when I walked out of Cage's bedroom at seven in the morning. And I really hadn't expected him to be standing at the stove cooking eggs and bacon.

"Good morning." I couldn't help but smile at how cute he looked cooking in a pair of sweats and T-shirt that covered his yummy chest I'd had a peek at last night.

"I didn't want you going to class hungry. So I figured since I was up, I'd go ahead and fix you something."

My heart melted a little. No one had ever made me breakfast. Not even my mother. Oh, fate really did suck. Why did this amazing, wonderful, sexy guy have to be a freaking Hardy? Why couldn't he be one of the guys from my neighborhood? Someone who understood the life I'd lived and didn't judge me or see me differently because of it?

"That's really sweet."

He grinned and reached for a plate. "Then I believe my mission is accomplished."

Laughing softly so I didn't wake up Cage, I walked over and took the plate he was offering to me.

"I made coffee, too. How do you drink it?"

This was really too good to be true. I glanced back at the bedroom door and wondered if I was actually still curled up in bed asleep. This was more dreamlike than the real world.

"Sugar? Cream?" His voice broke into my thoughts, and I turned my gaze back to him and smiled.

"Both, please. Two teaspoons of sugar. And thank you. Really. No one's ever made me breakfast before. I'm kind of at a loss for words."

His smile deepened, and there was something in his eyes I hoped I wasn't imagining. The interest was there. I could see it. Was it because he thought I was easy?

"You're welcome, and if you keep looking at me like that I may become your personal chef."

I covered the giggle I couldn't control. He was quite possibly the most charming guy I'd ever met.

His eyes got serious a moment, and I watched as he reached out and touched my cheek almost reverently.

"I really like your dimples," he whispered.

The heat rose up my neck so fast and flooded my face. I knew I had to look like a red berry. I hated my fair skin.

"Go sit down and eat, Low, please."

I obeyed without question.

I was on my second bite of eggs when he sat down across from me at the table.

"What class do you have today?"

I swallowed and took a drink of coffee to wash it down before responding.

"Calculus."

He grinned. "If you need any help, math is my thing."

I needed help but I doubted I'd be able to stop smelling him and ogling him long enough to pay attention to the words coming out of his mouth.

"Thanks."

He nodded and took a drink of his coffee.

"Are you coming back tonight?" he asked after a few minutes. I wanted him to be asking because he wanted to see me. But I also knew I needed to get those thoughts under control before I set myself up to get hurt.

"Not sure, but I doubt it. I'm probably going to stay at my sister's." I didn't want to elaborate, but I was due a night since I'd kept Larissa yesterday. Besides, I couldn't move in to Cage's bed.

A frown creased his forehead and he appeared to be thinking about something that bothered him.

"You know I don't mind you being here. If you need to stay here, I'm completely cool with it. This is Cage's place, after all."

I smiled and swallowed my last bite of bacon.

"Thank you but that isn't why. I can't just move in here. It would cramp Cage's style, and he'd eventually get annoyed with me. He doesn't see it that way, but I don't want to wear out my welcome."

Marcus shook his head. "You won't wear out your welcome. I'm positive Cage would never want you somewhere else. He's very protective of you."

I smiled and stood up to take my plate to the sink. "Whether he realizes it or not, he needs his freedom and room to breathe."

Marcus frowned but didn't respond.

"Thanks again for breakfast. It was the sweetest thing anyone has ever done for me. I appreciate it." The small frown eased at my words, and he smiled, but I could still see the concern in his eyes. God, he was going to get past my barriers. I needed to put some distance between us.

"I'm gone. See ya later," I called out as I headed for the door without looking back.

"Bye, Willow."

MARCUS

Amanda called me from school upset shortly after Willow left. Apparently Dad hadn't come home last night, and Mom had locked herself in her bedroom crying and wouldn't come out this morning. I'd gone by to check on Mom first, and she'd put on a happy face for me but the dark circles under her eyes told me she knew the truth. It was time I had a talk with Dad.

As I pulled into the parking lot at Sea Breeze High School, I spotted Amanda sitting on a picnic table outside the cafeteria entrance with Sadie White right beside her. Sadie's arm was wrapped around Amanda's shoulders as my sister cried. I wondered how much she had shared with Sadie. I hadn't seen or spoken to Sadie in over two months. I missed being around her, but it was just easier if I kept my distance. Sadie had been the one that got away for me. She'd been snatched out of my reach by a freaking rock star, as crazy as that sounds. Jax Stone, the hottest teen rock star in the world, had been both my and Sadie's employer last summer. We'd worked as staff in his summer home located on the private island connected to Sea Breeze. One look at Sadie and he'd been hooked. Unfortunately for me, she returned the feelings.

I parked my truck and headed over to get my sister. Sadie's concerned gaze met mine as I approached. I could tell by the look in her eyes she knew.

"Hey, Sadie, thanks for being here for her," I said as I walked up and reached out a hand to my little sister. She threw herself at me and began weeping harder. I wanted to kill my dad with my bare hands as her sobs shook her body. Damn him.

"She told me, Marcus," Sadie said quietly. "I'm sorry."

I nodded. "Yeah, me too. He's an ass. A selfish bastard."

Sadie didn't even flinch. She understood being furious with a parent. She'd had her hands full with her mother until Jax Stone fell in love with her and proceeded to fix all her problems. Sadie's spoiled, selfish mother, Jessica, had been one of the things he'd fixed.

"I just want to get away from it all. Can I come back to your place?" Amanda asked through her hiccups.

"Of course. Sadie, let the office know I have her, would ya?"

She nodded and stood up. "Of course. And, Marcus, if there is anything I can do, please don't hesitate to call me."

"Thanks, Sadie."

I pulled my sister up tightly against my side and headed back to my truck. First I'd deal with getting her calmed down, and then I was going to have a talk with my dad.

Chapter Four

WILLOW

My sister wasn't going to let me stay the night. I slipped my hand into the pocket of my jeans and squeezed the key Cage had given me. As much as I feared wearing out my welcome, I needed somewhere to stay. Besides, I'd left my suitcase in Cage's bedroom this morning. To pay him back for yet another night this week, I'd do our laundry this evening. Feeling somewhat better about being a freaking charity case, I headed for the stairs.

"Low, hey gorgeous, it's been too long." Preston flashed me his pretty-boy smile and tucked a strand of white-blond hair behind his ear. The boy knew his effect on females, but apparently he hadn't picked up on his lack of effect on me.

"Hello, Preston, and yes, it has. I'm surprised you're not around more now that your friend is living here."

A small frown puckered Preston's forehead. He glanced back up the steps at the door to the apartment, then turned back to me.

"Uh, yeah, well, about Marcus. He's having a bad day. His sister is up there, and she's really upset over some family stuff they've got going on. Why don't you and I go grab something to eat and head over to hear Jackdown play at Live Bay tonight. That is, if you're not working tonight. I haven't seen Dewayne and Rock in a while. I'm sure Dewayne would love to see you."

Going to listen to Jackdown wasn't what I needed to do tonight. I had a fair amount of homework, and tomorrow I would be working a double shift at the restaurant side of Live Bay. However, I also didn't want to intrude on a family problem. I knew enough about those kinds of problems to know Marcus needed some privacy.

"Um, okay, sounds good. Uh . . ." I glanced back toward the stairs. "Do you think maybe I could run in and change real quick? I'll just go straight to Cage's room and come right back out."

"Oh yeah, that's fine. I just meant they needed some time alone. They're probably in Marcus's bedroom anyway, and I doubt they'll even hear you come in. Come on, I'll go with you and grab a drink while you change."

I slipped my hand into my pocket and pulled out my key, feeling the strange warmth inside me at the sight of it. It was odd how something so small made me feel secure.

• • •

Once inside, I left Preston in the kitchen as I went into Cage's room. I could hear talking coming from behind Marcus's closed bedroom door as I passed by it. Maybe I could get out of here before they realized I'd come in. Marcus seemed okay with my being here a lot. I didn't want that to change.

I slipped into a short jean skirt and put on an emerald-green halter top, then pulled on the black leather jacket Cage had given me for Christmas two years ago. My cowboy boots sat in his closet lined up beside his, and I laughed at this small hint from Cage. He wanted me here. That much was obvious. The boy had no clue how impossible he made things.

Stepping out of the bedroom, I noticed Preston and Marcus whispering in the living room. I halted, not wanting to intrude, when Marcus's eyes met mine. Slowly his green eyes traveled down my body and back up, causing my pulse to race. I stood frozen in my spot until his eyes found mine again.

"Damn, girl, let's get your sexy ass out of here before Cage shows up," Preston said. "He'll have me hung up by my balls and you changing clothes while he stands guard at the door." His words were meant to break the silence, but they only made Marcus's eyes flare up.

"Um, okay, good idea." I forced a smile, and then willed my legs to move until I was beside Preston. His arm slipped around my shoulders, and he leaned his head down and sniffed me. "Mmmm . . . you even smell good."

Marcus cleared his throat loudly, causing Preston to chuckle.

"Go deal with Manda, bro. I just gave y'all the privacy you need. Cage has a date with some girl from Monroeville down here for spring break. And I intend to keep this one out late."

My face heated up at the insinuation in his voice. Surely Marcus knew I wasn't going to be out doing what Preston made it sound like I would be doing. What was wrong with him, anyway? He never laid his flirting on this thick.

"Good night, Marcus. I hope you get things worked out," I managed to say in a calm voice, with no hint of the frenzy his attention had sent my pulse into.

He nodded and turned around without a word.

MARCUS

Cowboy boots. Did she have to wear freaking cowboy boots with that tiny little skirt? I slammed the refrigerator door without getting a drink. A beer sounded really good after watching Preston walk out with Willow tucked against his side. But Amanda needed me. I couldn't drink even if right now all I wanted to do was get really trashed and forget this crazy mess my dad had laid in my lap.

"Why're you slamming things?" Amanda asked, stepping out of my bedroom.

I shrugged, not wanting to share with my sister how I was

having a small meltdown over a girl I'd just met while we had bigger issues to deal with.

"Does it have anything to do with the girl's voice I just heard in here with Preston?"

Slumping into a kitchen chair, I glanced up at her, intending to tell her no, but instead replied, "Yeah."

Amanda frowned at me and pulled the chair across from me out from under the table before sitting in it.

"Is Preston dating her?"

"No, not unless he has a death wish."

Amanda's eyebrows shot up in surprise. "You mean you like her enough to fight Preston over her?"

"Not me. Cage. He thinks he's going to marry Low."

Amanda laughed. "Cage, married? Has he gone from smoking pot to crack recently?"

It sounded ludicrous to me, too, but she hadn't seen him with Willow. He was different with her. He actually gave a shit.

"It's complicated."

Amanda picked at the red fringe on the place mat in front of her. The place mats were just another one of those small touches around this place that Willow had had a hand in. Preston was as bad as Cage when it came to women. I hated knowing he was out with Willow.

"I need to get home to Mom. I'd say you could come with me, but the awful scowl on your face would frighten her. You need to go get changed into something sexy and go after the girl. Preston wouldn't have taken her if he knew you liked her this much. Heck, he probably took her somewhere just to get her out of the apartment for our sake."

She was right. At least, I hoped she was right. I stood up and glanced down at the faded jeans and Alabama football T-shirt I had on.

"What's wrong with the way I'm dressed?"

Amanda sighed and stood up. "Come on, my clueless brother. I'll make you look irresistible. Trust me, okay? I mean the last girl you liked you completely let slip through your fingers. I'd say you need my help."

"I was up against a rock star, Manda. It wasn't exactly a fair fight."

Amanda shrugged. "Maybe so, but Preston and Cage are no Jax Stone. This time you're definitely the hottie in the group."

"Did you just call me a hottie? And Jax isn't better-looking than me. He's just famous."

Amanda let out a loud cackle of laughter.

"No, brother dear, Jax Stone is hotness incarnate with or without the guitar and sexy-as-hell singing voice. You never stood a chance. He was what you call playing with the big dogs. This time you're definitely playing within your league."

"Whatever. Just tell me what to wear and get out of here. You're pissing me off."

WILLOW

"You want a beer?" Preston asked, pushing us through the crowd of people toward a table with familiar faces.

"No thanks. But a Coke would be good," I replied loudly so he could hear me over the music. Jackdown hadn't taken the stage yet, but the band on before them had the crowd on their feet. From the sound of the band, it was probably the alcohol that had them all on their feet screaming and dancing. The band wasn't that good. Jackdown was the reason the crowd was here tonight. They always drew a crowd from the locals.

"Okay, go on over there and sit with Rock, Trisha, and Dewayne. I'll get our drinks and meet you there."

"Okay."

Rock and Dewayne were friends of Preston's I'd gotten to know through Cage over the past year. Trisha was Rock's wife. They reminded me of Kid Rock, with a shaved head, and Pamela Anderson. Trisha wasn't very natural, but she could definitely find success as a centerfold if she ever wanted to. That or an exotic dancer. Dewayne noticed me first, and a smile spread across his face. His long dreadlocks were pulled back in a ponytail tonight, and the shirt he was wearing was snug enough to show off his impressive chiseled body.

"Low!" Dewayne called out in greeting as I came up to their table. Trisha smiled brightly at me and gave me a small finger-wiggling wave. "Hey, girl. Didn't know you were coming tonight?

When we talked to Cage, he said he had some date tonight with a girl and he doubted they'd be leaving her hotel room."

Rock nudged Trisha and she flashed a frown at him. "What? Low isn't an idiot. The girl knows Cage is a slut."

"God, baby, drop it," Rock begged.

I shook my head and laughed, taking the chair beside Dewayne. "She's right, Rock. I know where he is and what he's doing. Just because he tells the world he's going to marry me doesn't mean I'm going to marry him. The boy is crazy. It doesn't bother me at all who he's with and what he's doing."

Rock nodded, and then a small frown creased his forehead. "So you came by yourself?"

"Nope, she's with me," Preston announced as he placed a Coke in front of me and took the chair on the other side of me.

"Ah, shit, man," Rock moaned, and Dewayne joined in with a frustrated sigh.

"What? Marcus and Manda were having some family issues, and he was dealing with her at the apartment. So I figured Low and I could come hang with you guys and hear Krit."

"Bad move," Dewayne mumbled before taking a swig of his beer.

"Whatever. Cage won't care. Besides he's out banging some girl tonight from Monroeville."

"As fascinating as this conversation is," Trisha said. "I think it's up to Low to decide what she does and who she does it with.

Cage isn't her daddy. Everyone stop acting like she belongs to him and let her have a life." Her annoyed tone shut everyone up, and I was grateful.

She stood up and held her hand out to me. "Come on, girl. You and I are going to go shake it out there and create a stir to give these boys something to do."

I frowned. "What will they do?"

She took my hand and pulled me up. "Threaten and scowl and possibly manhandle all the guys who're going to drool over us."

I could hear Rock's growl as we pushed our way into the crowd.

"Don't you get tired of everyone acting like you're Cage's property?" Trisha asked, pulling me closer to her as we made our way to the front of the crowd. Jackdown would be on in a few minutes, and I knew she was getting us to the front so we could see them. And so Krit could see me. She'd been trying to fix me and her brother up for months now. Cage always seemed to ice her attempts, but tonight Cage wasn't here.

"Cage is all I've got. He's my best friend and I overlook his issues. If a guy comes around worth fighting over, I won't let Cage stand in my way. But so far he hasn't kept me from anyone I really want."

Trisha studied me a moment. She didn't like my answer. I could see it on her face. "But if you don't date around, how will you know when the right one comes along?"

I shrugged, thinking about Marcus and pushing that thought immediately out of my mind. He was so not even close to my league. That was pointless to even fantasize about.

"I'll just know."

She shrugged and started to say something, but then the lights went down and the sound of Krit's electric guitar squealed out, sending the crowd into a frenzy of screams and cheers.

"Here we go," she replied, smiling and turning her attention to the stage. Smoke had engulfed it. Krit stepped out of the smoke into the single spotlight as he made his guitar sing. His long blond hair was so similar in color to Trisha's it made me think maybe hers wasn't out of a bottle after all. Instead of pulling his hair back, he let it fall down over his naked shoulders. Which was a trademark for Krit. He never wore a shirt onstage. The jeans he wore hung loosely on his hips, giving the females and probably some of the males a thrill from the small peek of hip bone he flashed. His chest wasn't as broad and muscular as Dewayne's and Rock's, but he had lean muscle and a very obvious six-pack that was covered on the right side by a coiled-snake tattoo.

The rest of the band stepped out of the smoke, and Green's voice joined the electric guitar. Green was Krit's best friend and the bass player slash alternate singer in the group. Krit was the lead singer, but Green could sing too, and he got several songs in each set. Green almost looked like Krit's dark-headed twin. The same long hair in a dark brown. Except Green wore a shirt of tattoos. His entire chest and arms were covered in tats. Looking at Green, one would never guess he was in his second year of law school. A girl to the right of me starting screaming his name along with a few rather colorful things she wanted to do to him after the show. Shaking my head to clear the mental images I so did not ask for, I glanced toward the back of the stage at the drummer, Matty. His bright-orange hair stuck straight up. It wasn't short, either. The guy had to use a ton of hair product to get that stuff to stick up like it did. His chest was covered by a tight black T-shirt, and although he was sitting behind the drums, I knew his jeans would be just as tight. The boy liked his skinny jeans.

"I can't wait until he sees you down here," Trisha squealed excitedly in my ear.

I really just wanted to dance. Getting Krit's attention was the last thing on my mind. I turned my attention toward the keyboard player, Legend. He was a hairy guy. He had a full-on beard, which was weird for a twenty-four-year-old guy, but he was proud of his hair. His shaggy brown hair was just long enough to tuck behind his ears, and his jeans hugged his hips tightly and hung low enough to show off his flat stomach where his tight Aerosmith T-shirt, which could have been mine it was so small, didn't meet his waist line.

Krit's voice joined in with Green's, and they began their most popular original song, "Aces."

Krit's bright blue eyes, which I once thought were enhanced by the help of contacts, found me. It seemed impossible for anyone's eyes to be that electric blue. Then I'd met Trisha and her's were the exact same color. Krit winked at me and licked his lips suggestively. I couldn't help but laugh. The guy was outrageous. Not my type at all, but very entertaining. His naked chest wasn't hard to look at either.

"I knew he'd love having you up close," Trisha yelled over the music. Smiling, I let my body move to the music.

After several songs and several dance partners, I made my way back through the crowd toward our table. My mouth felt like cotton. I needed my Coke even if it was probably watered down by this point. Preston was talking to a girl with wild curly brown hair. I smiled to myself, thinking I just might need to snag a ride home with Trisha and Rock.

Feeling eyes on me, I turned my attention to the other people at the table. Marcus was sitting in the chair Trisha had vacated earlier. I hadn't expected to see him here tonight.

"Hey," I said, walking up to the table, unsure where I should sit since the brunette talking to Preston was in my seat.

"Low, you're back." Preston stood up from his seat. "Here, sit down. You thirsty? Your ice melted. I'll get you another Coke."

"No, Preston, sit back down. I'm good. You continue your conversation. I'll go get my own drink." He didn't sit down, and his expression looked unsure. Chuckling at his obvious confusion, I turned and headed for the bar. Preston didn't just have pretty platinum-blond hair. He was really as air headed as one would imagine someone with his surfer-boy good looks to be.

"He doesn't seem to know any better. I'm sorry."

Marcus's voice was low and close to my ear. A shiver ran through me from the warmth of his breath tickling my neck. He'd followed me. The goofy smile on my face was unavoidable.

"Preston's a sweetheart. I overlook him. Besides, it isn't like I'm his date."

"You're not?"

I turned my head slightly so I could meet Marcus's gaze. "No, of course not. It's Preston. We're just friends."

A smile lifted the corners of Marcus's mouth, making it hard for me to look away. The boy was just downright sexy.

"Do you go out as friends with him often?"

"No. Not really. I mean, when I do I'm normally with Cage, too. But tonight he felt like you needed some alone time with your sister."

His smile vanished, and a frown replaced it as he nodded.

We reached the bar and Marcus came up behind me, caging me in with his arms on each side of me. The small thrill from his warm body pressing against my backside had me fighting the urge to snuggle in closer. I reminded myself that he was doing this to keep me from getting crushed in the sea of people swarming the bar. It was a protective gesture. Nothing more. But I liked it.

"Ricky! Two Cokes—make one a stiff."

The bartender looked our way, gave Marcus a short nod, and started fixing our drinks. That was quick service. It helped to be a local around here.

"When did you get here?" I asked Marcus as we waited on our drinks.

"About two minutes before you walked up. I was about to come find you and see if I could convince you to dance with me."

The acute sense of losing out struck me. Pressing against Marcus while we moved our bodies to the music would have ranked on my favorite moments in life list.

"Oh" was all I could manage in reply. My heart was racing from the fantasy playing out in my head. Being wrapped up in Marcus's clean, masculine scent didn't help matters. I was having a strange but oh-so-pleasing fantasy of crawling up under his shirt and licking his chest when our drinks were placed in front of us. Marcus slapped some money down and took our drinks. He nodded back toward our table, and I instantly missed his touch. Withholding my pathetic sigh, I led the way back to our friends.

Preston had moved the brunette to his lap, leaving me an empty seat beside the two of them. Awesome.

"I thought you were leaving," Marcus said to Preston as I sat down in the vacated seat.

Preston took a swig of his beer and glanced up at the girl

in his lap. Her red fingernails were playing with his silky blond locks.

"You going with me?" he asked her.

She giggled and nodded, sending her curls bobbing all around her shoulders. He looked around her at me. "Is it okay if I leave you with Marcus? He said he'd give you a ride home."

Yes! I managed to mask my pleasure at the change of plans and nodded. "Of course."

Preston grinned and stood up with his arm wrapped snugly around the girl's waist. "See y'all later."

I gave a small wave while I took a long drink of my Coke.

Rock was still on the dance floor with Trisha, and I had no idea where Dewayne had gone. It was just Marcus and me. Staring down at my glass of Coke and running my finger through the condensation trickling down the sides of it became fascinating, or so it would seem. I didn't know what to say and I suddenly felt awkward.

"Thanks for giving Manda and me some privacy today, but you don't ever have to feel like you can't stay at the apartment. No matter what's going on with me, you're always welcome."

I lifted my gaze from my glass and smiled at him. "Thanks. But I have family issues often, and I know privacy is always best."

He frowned and took a long sip of his drink, which I was pretty sure contained whiskey. "Well, I'll be having a lot of family issues over the next few months, so don't worry about me. If Manda shows up crying or is tucked away in my room, don't ever feel like you have to leave. Stay. I'd rather you stay than run off somewhere."

Had he come looking for me? Surely not.

"Thanks." I wasn't going to argue with him. Although if that happened again, I would not stick around and make them uncomfortable. But there was no point in arguing.

"Hey, bro! I didn't know you were here." Dewayne slapped Marcus on the back and took the chair beside me, grinning. "Day-um it feels good to have you showing up on a weekday. I miss your ugly mug when it's off at college." Dewayne, Rock, Marcus, and Preston had grown up together. According to Cage, they were all really tight. A strange combination, if you ask me. Marcus was the rich man's son, although he sure didn't live like it, and Rock owned his own parasailing company. Preston had no purpose in life but surfing, baseball, and girls, and then Dewayne was, well . . . I wasn't sure what he was. He looked dark and dangerous with tats and dreads, but his personality reminded me of a big teddy bear. He was always so nice and easy to talk to.

"I needed to get out and my roomies had both left me for the night, so I followed the pretty one here."

Did Marcus just call me pretty?

Dewayne chuckled. "Don't let Cage hear you call her pretty. He goes apeshit when guys mention Miss Willow's attractiveness." Dewayne winked at me and lit up a cigarette, leaning back in his chair.

"Cage is full of hot air," I assured them both, but mostly Marcus, who I did not want to scare off if there was any chance at all he might be interested in me.

Dewayne let out a laugh as smoke wafted out his nose and mouth. "Naw, baby, he's dead serious. I've seen him in action when someone said something about you. It ain't pretty."

Shut up, Dewayne. I glanced over at Marcus and he was frowning again. Dang it, I needed to stop Dewayne and his mouth.

"Marcus! Hey, you! I had no idea you were back in town. Why haven't you called me? I'm hurt." She was gorgeous. Figures: tall, blond, and all willowy. Just like the girls Cage is so fond of.

"Jess." Marcus stood up and hugged the girl. My insides cringed.

"Come dance with me," she pleaded, not letting go of her hold on him. She looked around him and smiled brightly at Dewayne. "Hey, D! How ya doin', baby?"

He nodded. "Good, Jess. You broke up with that wanker again?"

She scowled. "Yes, for over a month. He got someone pregnant this time. I can't forgive that."

Dewayne let out a low whistle. "Ouch . . . guess not. Daddy Hank. Never thought I'd hear that one."

She shrugged and pulled Marcus closer. "It's okay, I got me a handful of Marcus Hardy to make it all better," she cooed.

Marcus glanced down at me, and I forced a smile, then turned my attention to the stage, where Jackdown had just returned after their break. I couldn't watch him walk away with her. Seeing him with someone like her just reminded me of how out of my reach he was. "One dance," I heard Marcus say.

Jess squealed and led him into the crowd.

I will not think about it. I will not think about it.

"She's Rock's cousin. He couldn't turn her down." Dewayne's voice interrupted my mental chant. My face instantly heated at his words. He could tell it bothered me. Well, that was freaking perfect. Now I was really pathetic. The low-class plain Jane crushing on Marcus Hardy. Suddenly I wanted to leave. I wanted Cage. I needed to feel safe.

"Doesn't bother me. I didn't come here with him."

That didn't even sound believable. My voice had cracked, for crying out loud.

"Hmmmm," Dewayne said through drags off his cigarette.

"I need some fresh air and I need to make a phone call," I said, standing up. Dewayne raised his eyebrows and then nodded. I didn't need his all-knowing eyes on me. I headed for the door. Away from the warmth of the overcrowded bar and Dewayne's cigarette smoke blowing in my face.

Chapter Five

WILLOW

The night air was still cool. Even though our supershort spring weather was almost gone, our nights hadn't begun to warm up yet. I took a deep, cleansing breath of ocean air and stepped into the white sand, wishing I hadn't worn boots. I could have slipped off heels easily and felt the sand between my toes.

My phone rang in my purse and I pulled it out. It was Cage.

"Hey, you," I said, holding the phone pressed between my ear and shoulder as I walked down the beach toward our apartment.

"Where are you?"

Figures this would be his question. Knowing Cage, he was in the middle of sex and had realized he didn't know where I was tonight and had grabbed the phone to call me in between thrusts. Gross, bad mental image.

"Currently I'm outside Live Bay on the beach, getting some fresh air. Jackdown is playing tonight."

"Who's with you?"

"Well, I was with Preston, but he left with a girl, and Marcus said he would give me a ride home."

"Where's Marcus?"

"Inside dancing with a girl."

There was a pause.

"You ready to leave?" he asked.

I was, but telling Cage that would have him leaving his date and rushing to my side. He had a hero complex when it came to me. I often wondered if it was because no one had ever saved us as kids. No one had saved his mom when his stepdad beat her. He was just a kid, but I knew he blamed himself for not stopping it.

"I'm good."

"No, you aren't, Low. I can hear it in your voice. Something's wrong. I'll be there in five minutes."

"Cage don't—"

But he'd hung up. Oh well. No doubt the girl will let him come right back. They always did, which baffled me. If a guy ran off on me to go help some other girl while we were on a date I would not let him just run right back and jump into my bed later. But then, I wouldn't be having casual sex with a strange guy either. So this was a moot point.

Heading back up to the street, I glanced over at the lights

of Live Bay and figured I'd just call and let Marcus know I was leaving instead of going back inside. Besides, from the look of the blond bombshell in his arms, he probably wouldn't realize for a while that I was gone.

MARCUS

I finally managed to untangle myself from Jess. I wanted to dance with Willow. I'd watched her briefly when I'd first arrived, and all I could think about was being close to her and touching her while she moved like that. Jess had come along and delayed me. Dewayne sat at the table with Rock and Trisha. They were laughing and talking, but there was no Willow. I glanced toward the bar, but I couldn't see her in the crowd of people.

"Where's Willow?"

"What? No love for me first?" Rock taunted as he smirked up at me.

I turned to Dewayne. He was leaned back in his chair with a longneck beer in his hands as he watched me.

"Where's Willow?" I asked him specifically this time.

He flicked the metal bar in his bottom lip and tilted his head toward the door. "Went to get some air a while ago."

Oh no.

"How long ago?"

Dewayne seemed to be enjoying my frustration. He put a

stupid cigarette to his lips and took a long drag, then shrugged. "Since you ran off with Jess."

I'd turned to head outside when my phone rang. I hoped it wasn't Manda with another crisis concerning Mom right now. That was the last thing I needed. I had been making some headway with Willow. Until Jess had dragged me out onto the dance floor.

"Hello," I said, pressing the phone close to my ear as I stepped outside.

"I got my girl. I'm taking her home. In case you remembered you were her ride and couldn't find her later, I wanted you to know."

Cage had come to get Willow. *HELL!*

"Why, what's wrong? She okay?"

She'd called Cage to come get her, and he'd come to rescue her. Where had I been? Dancing. Perfect. Just perfect.

"She was just tired and ready for bed. Didn't want to bother you and your girl. I got her. All's good. Later, man." The phone call ended.

My girl? Jess was not my girl. I mean, I'd messed around with her in the past. She was Rock's hot little cousin but never anything serious.

I stood in the parking lot looking out at the cars. I'd screwed up already. Willow had all kinds of walls built around her. I wanted to get past them. I wanted her to trust me and let me in. But I'd let her down and she'd gone running to Cage. There had been interest in her eyes tonight. I'd seen it. I'd wanted to shout out loud in triumph at it. But then Jess had shown up, and I hated turning her down. Rock said she was going through a really bad time right now. All that had been about was trying to cheer up an old friend. Nothing more. But to Willow . . . it had looked like more. I'd left her. Cage had come for her. Who would have thought competing with Cage for the most trustworthy guy would be hard?

"You find her?" Trisha asked when I returned to the table. I needed another drink. This time screw the Coke. I just needed the whiskey.

"Cage got her."

Dewayne chuckled, and I shot him a warning glare. I didn't need to hear it from him right now. He always saw too much. Tonight I wanted him to keep his opinions to himself.

"Awww, dang. Krit wanted to come see her after this set."

I shifted my angry glare toward Trisha, who was grinning at me like she knew a hilarious secret.

"Hey, Hardy, don't look at my woman like that. Save your angry snarls for someone else." Rock's warning wasn't in jest. He meant business. I ran my hand through my hair and growled, looking back toward the door, wanting desperately to leave.

"She's got you all tied up in knots. It's about fucking time.

Sadie White did a number on you. Good to see you getting all worked up over another girl." There was no reason to deny Dewayne's observation. These were my best friends. They knew me better than anyone else. Lying to them was pointless.

"Why the hell does she run off to him all the time? I don't get it!"

Trisha set her drink down and leaned forward, staring directly at me. "Because he's her safe house. As screwed up as it is, considering who we're talking about. Cage cares about one thing in this world, and it's Low. He's been fighting her battles and fixing her problems since they were kids. We all lived on the same street. I remember watching them. It always fascinated me how bad-boy Cage York acted like a lovesick puppy when it came to her. She fell down, he came running. You want her, then good luck. Because every time you aren't there to pick her up, I can assure you Cage will be. She knows she can call him. She knows no matter what he'll love her. Unconditional love is hard to compete with."

I reached over and took a long swig of Dewayne's beer. Trisha was right. How did I compete with that? And did I even want to?

WILLOW

Cage closed the door behind us and threw his keys onto the table.

"I picked up some more of your Jarritos today. Go get you one while I get a shower."

I'd made Cage paranoid about the smells of perfume, sex, and whiskey that always clung to him after his dates. I wanted to tell him not to worry about it. I was fine, but I wanted alone time. So I nodded and headed for the fridge.

Cage kissed the top of my head on his way to the bathroom.

"I'll scrub up good. I promise," he called out as he closed the door.

I laughed quietly to myself and had started to go to his bedroom when the couch caught my attention. Memories of curling up against Marcus and waking up in his lap had me walking over to sit down on it instead. I liked it here. He sat here for hours letting me sleep in his lap. No one other than Cage had ever done something like that for me. Smiling, I took a sip of my drink. He was a good guy. A sexy guy. A fun guy to fantasize about.

My cheeks flushed at the thought that Dewayne may have told Marcus what he suspected. He suspected right. I was jealous. I liked Marcus way more than I should. But Marcus knowing was just embarrassing. My phone dinged, alerting me to a text message.

It was from Trisha.

"U make it home okay?"

I quickly typed:

"yes. Thank you =)"

"U r missed," she replied.

Missed by who? Marcus? Or just her? Surely Dewayne

hadn't discussed with everyone those unspoken words before I'd left. God, I hoped not.

I tucked my phone back inside my pocket and stood up. The shower had stopped and I wanted to get one next. Dewayne's cigarette smoke clung to my hair and clothes. I was exhausted and ready to put this night behind me.

I woke up before anyone else and collected Cage's and my dirty laundry and headed to the laundry room downstairs to get started on it. Cage had crawled into bed beside me last night, and we'd gone to sleep without many words. He didn't get up and leave all night, which meant he was resting up for a reason. Today had to be a game day. And his uniform was dirty as were all my clothes and most of his jeans. I added bleach to the water and threw his filthy, dirt-stained uniform in by itself. Luckily, there were three washers and dryers down here and all three were empty. Many of the apartments had their own, so rarely did I come down here and find someone else using them. It made laundry time go so much quicker. Once I got all three machines going, my phone rang. Pulling it out of my pocket, I glanced down to see it was Tawny. She never called me, and when she did it was never good.

"Hello."

"Where are you?"

"At Cage's."

"Figures. Listen, I need a sitter for tonight. I have a date.

Larissa is asking for you. If you keep her, then you can stay the night. I probably won't be home until the morning anyway."

"I've got work, Tawny."

"Shit. Fine. If I have to pay a sitter, then don't come back here this week."

"I wasn't planning on it."

"What, you've finally shacked up with Cage? Just like our mama."

"No, Tawny, *you* are just like our mama. I'm still a virgin, and you have a kid and no husband. Do the math, sister."

"Whatever. Bye."

The call ended. I felt sick to my stomach at the thought of Larissa being left overnight with some sitter. There was no telling who Tawny would get. I dialed her number back.

"What?"

"After work I'll come over and keep her overnight. Don't get a sitter for all night."

There was a brief pause.

"Okay, fine. What time do I tell the sitter you'll be here?"

"I work a double, but I'll get someone to switch with me so I can leave by eleven. So tell her eleven thirty. I may have to walk."

"Fine."

She hung up again.

If it wasn't for my niece, I doubt I'd even talk to my sister. There was no love between us, and I wasn't sure why. When we were little,

I'd tried so hard to gain her approval, but nothing I did pleased her. It was as if my being born had ruined her life. Who was I kidding? My mother acted the same way. My birth had not been cause for celebration for anyone in my family. Some days I imagined getting on a bus and leaving this town behind. The memories weren't good. At least, most of them weren't. I could fit my life into one suitcase. The only person who would miss me would be Cage. Well, and Larissa until she forgot I existed. Just starting over anywhere else was so tempting. Eventually Cage would see the wisdom behind my leaving. He'd be free of his need to protect me. I'd make new friends. Maybe find a decent job and finish my education.

"Deep thoughts?" Marcus's voice startled me, and I jerked my gaze up from the cement floor to stare up into sleepy green eyes.

"Hey. What're you doing down here so early?"

He shrugged and set a basket of laundry down on the floor beside him. "Well I thought I'd get some laundry done before I fixed breakfast. But it appears all the machines are in use." His tone was teasing.

"Oops. Sorry about that. I didn't think anyone would need them so early."

"That was my thought too."

I let out a small laugh and fiddled with my thumbs while my hands fisted nervously in my lap. Did he know I'd run out like a jealous idiot last night?

"So, you left me last night." His tone didn't give anything away.

I tucked the hair acting as a wall between us behind my ear.

"Um, yeah. Sorry. I was tired and needed some air."

He didn't respond right away, and I prayed my breathing was normal, because my heart was doing a strange little fluttery thing.

"I would've taken you home if I'd known you wanted to go."

Because he was one of the good guys.

"You were having fun. Your friends obviously miss you. I didn't want to ruin your night. Cage was coming my way, so it worked out okay."

A small frown touched his lips, and I turned my eyes back to the cement crack in the floor I'd been staring at before he'd arrived.

"I was enjoying your company too. I'd looked forward to taking you home."

Okay, now the fluttery thing my heart was doing had turned into a full-blown pounding.

Had Marcus Hardy just insinuated he was upset because he hadn't gotten to take me home?

"Oh," I responded. What else did I say to that?

The first washer stopped, and I jumped up and made myself busy putting the load in the dryer.

"Washer is free," I announced, smiling back at him.

He stood up, and instead of waiting on me to move out of

the way, he crowded me back against the washer and set his basket on the closed washer beside it. I lifted my eyes up to his to say "Excuse me," but the heated look in his green eyes stopped me. A small gasp left my mouth.

"I don't think I'm making myself very clear, Low." He'd lowered his voice, and the effect made chill bumps break out over my body. "I was only interested in one person at that bar last night. I only came to see one person." He tucked a strand of hair behind my ear and softly caressed my earlobe before tracing the line of my jaw. "I was there for you."

The husky whisper in his voice made it hard for me to take a deep breath. Instead, I was making small little pants.

"Oh," I whispered.

He chuckled and lowered his head until his lips were hovering over mine.

"*Oh!* Ah, um, I, uh . . ." The startled female voice broke the spell, and Marcus closed his eyes tightly and cursed. Straightening up, he turned around to face whoever had entered the room. I couldn't see over his back, and from the way he was keeping me cornered with his body I realized he didn't want the intruder to see me either. At least not my face.

"Sadie?" I could hear the surprised confusion in his voice.

"Uh, Marcus, I'm so sorry. I was headed up to your apartment and I saw the back of your head through the window and came in. I didn't see anyone else."

"No, it's okay. What're you doing here?" Marcus's body was strung tight as a bow. Something was off with this situation. Who was Sadie?

"It's Amanda. She stayed over at my place last night. I took her home this morning, and your mom was, well . . . Anyway, uh, she's outside in the Hummer and upset. I didn't know what else to do." The sound of the girl's musical voice was not helping my imagination. She had an odd effect on Marcus.

"No, you did the right thing. I'm coming."

I heard the door shut, and Marcus let out a defeated sigh.

"I gotta go check on her."

"Of course you do." I stepped out from around him this time and went to the other washing machine, which had stopped, to unload it.

He stared at me as if he was going to say something else, but instead shook his head and left the room, his dirty laundry forgotten.

I got my other two loads in the dryer, then put a load of his dark clothes in to wash.

Standing in the washroom without Marcus suddenly felt cold and lonely. He'd almost kissed me. He'd come to see me last night. But then Sadie had shown up. She affected him. Why? Jess, Sadie . . . there were many girls in his life. Just like Cage. I shook my head and cleared my thoughts. I needed to finish up and get ready for work.

Chapter Six

MARCUS

Sadie was twirling a strand of her blond hair around her finger. She did that a lot when she was nervous. "I am so sorry I walked in on that, Marcus. I feel like an idiot," she began explaining as soon as I made it to Jax Stone's Hummer.

"No worries." Which wasn't exactly the truth. Sadie walking in on me about to kiss Willow had screwed with my head a little. Sadie had had me wrapped so tightly around her finger not too long ago that I'd expected to feel something when, with Willow's warm body pressed against my back, I turned around and saw her standing there. But I hadn't. Nothing. No ache at the sight of her. Absolutely nothing. Righteous anger at my father and the hell he was putting my mom and sister through—yes, I'd felt that. Worry for Amanda—yes, I'd felt that. But nothing for Sadie. My immediate response was to protect Willow. Not sure what I was protecting her from, but nonetheless that had been my goal.

Sadie opened the door, and Amanda sat curled up in the corner sniffling like a little girl. My heart broke. It was like I'd stepped back in time and the little sister I loved and protected needed me to fight off the monsters under her bed again. But this time the damn monster was our father. He was ripping us apart for a twenty-year-old whore. Or however old she was. She was young. That's all I knew.

"He didn't come home last night, and Mama won't come out of her room. She's screaming and packing her things. She's running away." A choked sob escaped her, and she buried her face in her hands again. My spoiled, sweet little sister hadn't ever had to deal with life's shit. She'd been given everything she wanted. Her life had been cake and ice cream until now.

"Come on, baby, I'm going to talk to Mama, and I'll get her calmed down. She isn't going to run away. I promise."

"She can stay with me if you need her to," Sadie said. "We've already missed an hour of school. Might as well make it a day."

I glanced over at Sadie and nodded. That was probably a good idea. Amanda didn't need to hear what I had to say to Mama.

"You want to stay with Sadie while I go handle Mama?"

She nodded slowly, looking up at me with a tear-streaked face.

I leaned inside and hugged her. "It's going to be okay, sis. I'm here, and no matter what, I will fix this mess."

"'Kay," she muttered against my chest.

I knew I was making a promise I might not be able to keep, but I'd said it anyway.

"Thanks, Sadie," I said, letting go of Amanda and stepping back so Sadie could climb inside the Hummer. Jax supplied a Hummer and a chauffeur for Sadie complete with black privacy windows. Since the world had found out Sadie White was Jax Stone's girlfriend, she'd become a celebrity. Paparazzi actually came to Alabama to get pictures of her. People treated her differently when she went out in public. Jax didn't like being away from her and left her with several things that made him feel she was safe. The Hummer and chauffeur/bodyguard were just two of them. Why the dude didn't just get her a private tutor and take her with him was beyond me. Something about not wanting to take away her high school experience or some crazy shit. Only a guy who had never lived through high school would feel like he was robbing someone of the experience. Sadie would leave in a heartbeat if he'd let her.

"I'm glad I can help. Anything y'all need from me, I'm more than willing to help out. I hate that this is happening. Amanda's tears are breaking my heart."

Sweet, kind Sadie. I expected nothing less. It was one of the reasons I'd fallen head over heels for her after only minutes in her presence last summer. She was gorgeous, sure, but the girl was also a sweetheart. However, I had to admit that standing here talking to her and feeling nothing but gratitude was pretty damn freeing.

"You're an awesome friend, Sadie," I said, nodding and then left as she climbed inside beside my sister.

I needed to go deal with my mother.

The Mercedes CLS63 my dad had given my mother as an anniversary present four months ago was still sitting in the garage. This was a good thing. She hadn't taken flight yet. I headed inside the three-story stucco beachfront home I'd lived in my entire life. "Mom," I called out as I headed for the stairs leading to her room.

"Marcus," she called back, followed by a loud wail. The little boy in me took off running up the stairs, scared of what I might find. She was my mom. I didn't want her hurt. As my foot hit the top stair, she flung herself out of her bedroom and threw herself into my arms.

"You're here," she sobbed out.

I stroked her blond hair gently, hoping to calm her down. How many times had she held me while I cried in her arms? I couldn't even begin to count. Now here I stood holding her.

"He didn't come home last night," she sobbed. "He didn't even call."

I hated him. At this moment with my mother sobbing pitifully in my arms, I knew I hated him. I didn't just hate what he was doing. I truly hated my father.

"I know. Manda told me. Come with me. Let's get you a wet washcloth for your face and clean you up a little." She nodded against my chest and relaxed the deathlike grip she'd had on me.

"Go sit down on the sofa, Mama. I'll get you a cool wash-cloth, and then we can talk about this and what we need to do. Okay?" She let out another sob.

"I'm here, Mama. I won't leave you. I'm going to fix every-thing. You just trust me, okay?"

A small smile of relief mixed with misery tugged on her lips. The pain in her eyes, however, didn't lessen.

I was going to kill him. With my bare hands. I was going to kill my father. And God help me if that slut who works for him ever comes near me. I can still remember that flirtatious smile she shot me when I'd gone into his office that day. She was a gold digger. And my dad was a sucker. A selfish sucker.

"I called his cell phone this morning and he answered. Said he was at work and would deal with me later." She let out a choked laugh. "Deal with me, Marcus. Like I'm a problem. I'm his wife. His *wife*."

I sat down beside her and used the washcloth to clean her tear-streaked face.

"Just don't call him anymore. I'm going to go talk to him. I want him out of this house, Mama."

She sniffed, sitting still while I washed her face as if she were the child.

"You think I should divorce him?"

"Yes, Mama, I do. He's sleeping with someone else. He doesn't deserve you. You're better than that."

She nodded and reached up to grab my wrist and pulled my hand to her mouth and kissed it. "I love you, Marcus Hardy. You're my good boy. Always taking care of me and your sister. You're nothing like your daddy. You know that, don't you?"

There was my mom. Even if it was for a brief moment, I needed that little bit of motherly affection. Knowing she was still in there under all this hurt and pain eased my fear some.

"I know that," I assured her, allowing her to take the washcloth from my hand so she could wipe her nose.

"God, Marcus, how did this happen? Where did it all go wrong?" she asked in a defeated tone, dropping her hands into her lap.

"The minute Dad lost his mind, I guess. I'm going to go talk to him. Don't wait up for him tonight, Mama. I'm going to tell him I'll bring him his clothes but I don't want him back on the property."

"Oh, honey, is that the best idea? What if he realizes this was a mistake? Do I really just end twenty five years of marriage over this?"

"Yes, Mama, you do! The bastard cheated on you. He is

cheating on you. You're so much better than that, Mama. Don't you let him win. Don't do it."

I hated seeing her this way. She really thought Dad would change his mind and come back to her. Maybe he would when his little girlfriend left him or began to get on his nerves. But then there would be another one just like her somewhere waiting to take her place.

"Mama, listen," I pleaded, taking her cold, soft hands in mine. "You need to divorce him. Take everything you possibly can by law. Clean him dry. Do you hear me? He is using his money on that slut. Get what he owes you, and he owes you everything, Mama."

She straightened up and nodded in agreement. Thank God I'd gotten through to her.

"You're right, honey. I need to make him pay."

Good. I could see the revenge flashing in her eyes. At least it wasn't pain. Let her be mad as hell. Let her suck him dry. That's the tough-as-nails woman who raised me. I leaned over and kissed her on the cheek. "I love you, Mama. We're going to get through this. You're not alone. Don't push Manda away either. She needs you right now. The two of you need to eat a gallon of Rocky Road ice cream and watch movies together. Bond over this, Mama. Don't let him win."

Standing up, Mama reached out and squeezed my hand.

"You're right. I'm stronger than this. My baby girl needs her

Mama. As long as I have you to lean on, I can do this, Marcus."

"Well, you've got me. Now, why don't you get out of your paja-mas and come make me some breakfast? Because I'm starving."

Her laughter was music to my ears.

WILLOW

It was spring break season, so the tourists had begun flood-ing Sea Breeze. Which was a good thing because tips were double their norm. I'd already made two hundred dollars, and that was mostly from the lunch crowd. The evening crowd was just beginning to pick up. On nights when the bar side of Live Bay has a relatively known band, the restaurant suffers some. Families looking for a nice seafood restaurant are put off by the packed parking lot. They don't realize it's for the bar side. Tonight, however, the bar wasn't crowded, so the restaurant was hopping with tourists.

"Low, can you take a four-top in section C for Macy? She said she can't handle any more in her section. That twelve-top party is consuming her."

I nodded at Kim, the hostess for the evening, and went to grab some waters and a bowl of lemons before heading to their table.

"Hey, you still looking for someone to close for you?" she asked me as I turned to walk away. I glanced back at her. "Yep."

She pointed to Seth, a waiter who I knew she'd been seeing lately. She must've wanted him to work late with her tonight.

Giving her a knowing smile, I headed over to intercept Seth on his way to the kitchen.

"Hey, you want to close tonight? I've got to keep my niece, and I need someone to close for me."

Seth glanced back over his shoulder toward Kim. Apparently he was looking for her approval before answering. His gaze shifted back to me and he grinned.

"Sure. No problem." His obvious enthusiasm had me biting back a laugh. No doubt he was already planning his evening alone with Kim in a big empty restaurant.

"Hey, isn't that the lead singer of Jackdown?" Seth asked.

I looked over and, sure enough, sitting at my four-top in section C were Krit, Trisha, Rock, and Green.

"Yep, and the bassist, too."

"Switch with me, please," Seth begged.

I glanced back at the table and Trisha waved. I couldn't do that to her.

"I would, Seth, but Trisha and Rock are my friends. I can't."

Seth's eyes widened. "You know Krit, then?"

"Yep."

"Well then, can you at least introduce me? I've been wanting to audition for Jackdown for forever, but they're never looking for anyone new."

He was helping me out tonight so I really owed it to him. Even though he would no doubt be getting lucky back in the stockroom tonight with Kim.

"Sure, stop by after I've got their orders and I'll introduce you."

Carrying a tray full of waters, I headed back to my newest table.

"Hey, girl, hate you left early last night. You missed the last song. Krit wrote it, and it was amazing," Trisha said, smiling up at me.

"I'm sorry. It was just once I got outside in the clean air, I couldn't bring myself to go back inside into that crowd." Not to mention I didn't want to see Marcus dancing with Jess.

"You broke my heart. I was looking forward to the end of my set so I could come find you. The boots and miniskirt were hot, Low, you were killing me."

"She had on a miniskirt and boots? How, exactly, did I miss this?" Green asked, looking from me to Krit.

I laughed and pulled out my order pad.

"What can I get y'all to drink?" I asked, changing the subject.

"Bud on tap," Rock replied.

"Diet Coke."

"Miller Lite longneck."

"Sweet tea."

I wasn't twenty-one, and even though it was legal for me to serve alcohol at nineteen, the owner didn't like it. He preferred to have those old enough to consume it serve it. This would be the perfect reason to get Seth to the table.

"I'll have Seth bring y'all your beers since I'm not allowed to serve you. But be prepared, he's a huge Jackdown fan and really wants to meet y'all."

Krit leaned forward and bit his bottom lip while staring me down. He really did think his sex appeal worked on everyone.

"What time do you get off, Low?" he asked in a husky voice.

"Ah shit, he's already using his 'fuck me' voice on her. Run, Low, before he starts the winking and dimple flashing," Green warned, then gave Krit a playful punch in the arm when everyone at the table burst into laughter.

"I'll go get the other drinks," I said, smiling as I turned back toward the kitchen.

Seth was at the soda fountain filling up two glasses.

"All right, I need a Bud on tap and a Miller Lite longneck delivered to the table. The Miller is Krit's. Enjoy."

"Awesome, Low. Thanks." Seth rushed off, leaving the sodas behind.

Krit's flirting proceeded throughout the meal, but I was used to flirtatious customers, so it didn't bother me. When I knew they were getting to the end of their meal, I printed out their check and started to make my way over to them. But before I could take another step, the front door opened and I halted. The small audible gasp that escaped me luckily went unnoticed since no one was close enough to hear it. Walking through the door was a very gorgeous and very determined-looking Marcus Hardy. His blond hair was short enough that it didn't require much brushing, and although he pulled off the just-got-out-of-bed style with ease, tonight his hair had been paid attention to. The short blond locks were neatly in place, with the front flipped up just barely. The jeans rode low on his hips, hugging them in just the right spot, and the pale-green polo he had on made his green eyes stand out even more under his heavy eyelashes.

He nodded at Kim but kept his eyes on me as he headed directly to where I stood frozen in place.

"I heard you needed a ride tonight," he said with a pleased expression on his face.

"I do, um, but how did you know?" The twinkle in his eyes made me feel warm all over.

"I have my sources. Didn't want you walking or being stranded, so I thought I'd come grab a drink and wait until you're ready to go."

I had planned on walking to my sister's. Cage had a game tonight and I hadn't wanted to ask him to let me borrow his car.

"Well, okay, um, thank you. Rock's here," I said, trying to process the fact that Marcus had just shown up to take me to my sister's after work as if this was normal behavior.

He followed my gaze. "I see that. I'll go say hello to them.

Take your time. I have nowhere to be. I've got all night."

With one last long look directed at me, he turned and walked to the table I'd been heading to before he walked in. How the heck had he known I needed a ride? And furthermore, why would he come to give me one without me asking him?

Shaking my head in confusion, I followed him to the table.

"Marcus, man, you missed the meal," Rock teased.

"Yeah, I can see that, but I'm here for Low, not you."

Krit glanced past Marcus and locked eyes with me. His blond eyebrows shot up in question at Marcus's comment.

"You taking Low somewhere, Marcus?" Krit asked, tearing his gaze off me and staring back up at Marcus.

This might get more interesting than was good. I'd been dodging Krit's advances for almost a year. The boy didn't take no for an answer.

"Yep, you got a problem with that?" Marcus asked, pulling up a chair and sitting down beside Green.

"I guess I do. I'd been hoping to convince her to go out with me when she got off work tonight. Kinda screws that up if you're here for her."

I couldn't help but watch Marcus's face to see how he reacted to Krit's explanation. He scowled and leaned back in the chair.

"No, I don't think that's a good idea, Krit. You aren't Low's type."

"And you are?"

I couldn't bring myself to walk completely up to the table. This was as embarrassing as it was fascinating.

"All right, boys, calm down," Rock interrupted them, and waved me over. "I'm gonna pay for this meal, and Krit, you're going to leave with us. Low has plans tonight to leave with Marcus. You two can argue this out or beat the shit out of each other or whatever some other time. Right now I want to get home and spend some time with my girl, alone."

Marcus looked entirely too pleased with everything. If he wasn't so darn cute, I'd remind him I wasn't some piece of property he owned. Heck, we hadn't even been out on a date and here he was acting like he had some claim on me.

His eyes lifted and locked with mine. All the reasons I had to be aggravated with him vanished. Who could stay mad at that face?

Chapter Seven

MARCUS

Willow didn't say much on the ride to her sister's house. I wasn't sure if she was mad at me about the confrontation I'd had with Krit or what, but she was quiet. I hadn't meant to step out of bounds with her. Just the thought of Krit taking advantage of her or treating her like I knew he treated women made my skin crawl. Low was too sweet for someone like him. She needed someone to handle her gently.

"Look, I'm sorry about what I said to Krit. It isn't my business who you date. I was out of line."

Not that I wouldn't do it again if I had to, but I wanted to see her smile at me. She would be getting out of my truck in just a few minutes, and I needed the sound of her laughter to keep me warm tonight.

"You were out of line. But you were right. Krit isn't my type. I've been dodging him for a while now."

Good. She knew he was an asshole.

"So do you forgive me?" I asked, glancing over at her.

A small smile lifted the corners of her lips.

"Yes, I suppose I do."

I let out a dramatic sigh of relief.

"Dang, girl, you had me sweating over here."

The laughter I'd wanted to hear filled the truck. My chest expanded and I suddenly wanted to beat on it with my fist. The girl was making me go all caveman.

"I'm sorry I worried you. I'm just tired tonight. It's been a long day."

"Will you be able to go straight to bed when you get there?"

I didn't like the idea of leaving her at her sister's. I was growing accustomed to knowing she was safe and sound in the apartment at night.

"I'll get a shower first, but then, yes, I'll go right to bed." She shifted in her seat and turned her head toward me. "Is everything okay with your sister?"

The memory of our almost kiss made me desperate to pull over and finish what was interrupted this morning.

"She's fine. Thanks."

"Good."

I waited, hoping she'd bring up the kiss, but she didn't.

Instead, we drove the rest of the way in silence. When she pointed to the small cinderblock house, I pulled into the driveway. Wishing there was some way to keep her with me.

"This is it," she said with a sleepy tone to her voice. Unbuckling her seat belt she reached for the handle on the door, then glanced back at me. "Thank you for the ride tonight. I don't know how you knew I needed a ride, but I'm very thankful you showed up. I'm exhausted, and walking would have sucked."

I'd overheard Cage talking to her earlier on the phone. I knew from his end of the conversation that she needed a ride tonight but that she was going to get one from a coworker. I figured she was either telling Cage a lie to appease him and needed a ride, or she had a ride but would cave in and let me take her home if I just showed up. I'd been pretty dang determined when I'd walked into the restaurant tonight that I would be walking out with Low beside me.

"Yeah, well, I got my ways. But you know, it would be easier on my superhuman powers if you'd call me next time. That way I won't have to use my mind reading skills."

She giggled. "Okay, I'll do that. I wouldn't want to be the cause of you overusing your superpowers."

"My thoughts exactly. It would be incredibly helpful."

Her laughter faded, and she smiled at me, then turned and stepped out of the truck.

I thought about walking her to the door, but then I'd kiss

her, and suddenly that first kiss had become incredibly important. I didn't want it to be outside her sister's house, somewhere
she hated. I wanted it to be somewhere she'd remember fondly.
So instead, I watched her until she was safely inside before I
backed out of the drive and headed home.

WILLOW

When I got my hands on Tawny, I was going to strangle her. No
strangling would be too good for her. I was going to pull out her
hair one strand at a time. No, I was going to pull it out in large
handfuls at a time. How were we even related? If it wasn't for the
fact that we shared the same exact hair color as our mother, then
I'd swear I was switched at birth. What crazy mother doesn't come
home in time to get her baby, or even call? I mean, really! Who
does that? I shifted Larissa up higher on my hip and carried her
diaper bag on my other arm. Her car seat sat on the gravel road
beside my feet. The child required more stuff just to go somewhere than I actually owned. Kissing her sweet head, I snuggled
her close to me. I refused to leave her with the crazy cat lady when
I knew good and well my sister didn't have to work today.

Cage pulled up beside me before jumping out of the car and
running around to help me with Larissa and her bag.

"Here, I'll buckle her car seat in."

Cage had become a pro at car seat installation since Larissa
was born. More times than not he'd had to come to our rescue.

He turned around and took Larissa out of my arms, "Hey, baby girl," he cooed at her while cradling her in his arms. She loved Cage. The girl was a sucker for men. Especially attractive men. Bless her heart, she took after her mama. Her pudgy hand reached up and patted his cheek. "Cay," she announced loudly. She'd recently started calling him Cay. She hadn't mastered the *g* sound yet.

"Yep, Cage has got his girl. Now come on, let's get you buckled up."

Once he had her secured, he stood up and pulled me into his arms.

"Bad morning?" he said, rubbing my back. I simply nodded and let him comfort me. He was so good at it. "It's okay now. I got ya. Let's get Squirt to the apartment, and then we'll worry about finding her mama. Tawny is bound to show up sometime today."

"Yes, but I'm missing classes because she didn't show up on time," I grumbled.

"She's a selfish bitch. This isn't anything new. You know that."

With a defeated sigh I sank down into the passenger seat of Cage's black Mustang and laid my head back on the seat. I was still tired. Larissa had woken up at four with a bellyache and then again at six. I needed more sleep than that. It probably would have been pointless to go to class today anyway. I wasn't sure I could have kept my eyes open while listening to a lecture.

"She keep you up a lot last night?"

I nodded while yawning.

"I'd say I'd watch her for you at the apartment so you could sleep, but I can't miss class or I'll have to sit out a game."

"I know. I'll crash after Tawny gets her. Good news is, I don't work tonight."

Cage turned on the radio and we drove back to the apartment in comfortable silence.

MARCUS

I'd been awake since I'd heard Cage leave. It was too early for him to be up, especially since he got in so late last night. Which could only mean one thing. Willow had called him. After last night, I'd hoped she'd call me the next time. Apparently not.

I'd just finished making another pot of coffee when the door opened. Cage came walking in. A little girl with short blond ringlets bouncing around her head was in his arms. Big green eyes, bright and excited, scanned the apartment before they landed on me. Willow stepped in behind them, carrying a large pink polka-dot bag, and dropped it on the chair beside the door. She wore tiny shorts I remembered the cheerleaders wearing back in high school when they practiced. Those shorts were meant to drive guys crazy. The blue hoodie she was wearing had HURRICANES BASEBALL on the front, and it was entirely too big for her. I'd seen Cage in it more than once.

"I'll go get the car seat out of the car and bring it up. Then I gotta change and go," Cage told Willow.

She covered her mouth to stifle a yawn. Last night must not have gone well.

"'Kay, thanks," she replied, then reached for the little blonde who clung to Cage's shirt. "Come on, Larissa, let's get you some breakfast. Cage has to go to school."

The little blonde patted Cage's chest. "Cay."

"Yes, that's Cage. Now kiss him good-bye and come with me."

She turned and gave Cage a very loud, wet kiss on his face that looked like it may have had a little licking involved.

Cage laughed. "Now, that's the way to start a guy's day, Larissa."

Holding out her pudgy little arms, she went to Willow.

"Good morning, Marcus," Willow said as she walked into the kitchen with Larissa.

"Bad night?"

She shrugged and a little frown puckered her brow. "You could say that. Larissa, this is my friend Marcus. He lives with Cage now." She looked from the little girl to me. "Marcus, this is my niece, Larissa."

I set my coffee cup down and reached out to take her little hand in mine and shake it.

"It's very nice to meet you, Larissa."

She burst into a fit of high-pitched giggles and clapped when I let her hand go.

"She's a flirt, so beware," Willow warned, and walked over to the table. I watched as she set Larissa in a chair, then squatted down so she was eye level with the little girl. "I can make you pancakes or eggs, or if you want, I bet Cage would let you have some of his Cocoa Puffs."

Larissa nodded happily.

"Okay, I'm not making you all three. You've got to pick one. Pancakes, eggs, or cereal."

Larissa's expressive eyes met mine, and she grinned. The kid was adorable.

"Cay's cedeul."

I nodded and stood up. "Cage's cereal it is."

Her shoulders were slumped under the oversize hoodie and there were circles under her eyes. I didn't like her being so tired.

"I've got it. You sit down with Larissa, and if you're really good I'll make you an omelet."

She stopped and tilted her head to the side and studied me. I held her gaze.

"Why?"

I closed the distance between us and reached up to gently rub my thumb over the dark circles under her eyes.

"Because you're exhausted. Because I want to. Because I'm

90

trying really hard to get you to trust me."

Her breathing hitched, and at that moment I wanted to forget Cage was in the other room and there was a little blond doll sitting over in the chair watching us. All I wanted was to kiss her. Instead, I dropped my hand and stepped back.

"Okay," she said in a small, breathy voice.

"Good. Now go sit down and let me fix you some coffee."

She nodded and obediently went and sat down next to Larissa.

"Martus," Larissa announced, and then proceeded to clap loudly.

I glanced at the table while I poured Willow's coffee.

Willow was grinning at me. "I do believe you've been awarded the honor of Larissa adding your name to her limited vocabulary."

So Larissa liked me. I winked at her and she giggled again, clapping her small, pudgy hands. I wished her aunt was that easy to win over.

Reaching into the fridge, I grabbed the gallon of chocolate milk my mom had sent home with me along with a few bags of groceries yesterday. Grabbing a sports bottle out of the cabinet, I poured some chocolate milk into it and walked it over to the table with Willow's cup of coffee.

"Here ya go, ladies. Coffee for the gorgeous redhead and chocolate milk for the beautiful blonde."

"Choctate! Lowlow! Choctate!" Larissa squealed excitedly.

Willow chuckled, then looked up at me and gifted me with a full-on smile.

"Thank you."

I was making progress. Nodding, I headed back to the fridge to whip up a bowl of cereal and an omelet.

"Low, can I have my hoodie, or do you need it? I can't find my leather jacket." Cage came walking out of his bedroom, interrupting my time with the girls. I'd almost forgotten he was still here.

Willow stood up and pulled the hoodie off. I almost dropped the eggs. She was wearing a tight black tank top that didn't reach her belly button.

"No, you can take it. All my clean clothes are here."

Cage walked up to her and grabbed it, bending down to kiss her on the cheek, then giving Larissa the same attention.

"All right, girls, be good. Larissa don't give Low a hard time, okay?"

Larissa stared up at Cage, smiling, but she didn't agree to anything.

"Be careful," Low called out as Cage headed for the door.

"Always," he responded, then left.

I didn't let myself look back at Willow. She really needed to put on a shirt. One that didn't show me her smooth, flat stomach and perfect little belly button.

Her phone started to ring and she grumbled, "Finally," then

stood up and walked toward the living room before answering.
"Where are you?

"I had class this morning, Tawny. You didn't even call me.

"No, I'm at Cage's.

"Because there wasn't even milk at your house. Larissa was starving.

"She's about to eat now.

"Well when will you be here?

"I'm exhausted, Tawny.

"Whatever.

"No!

"Okay fine. Just please go get some food first."

Willow growled before walking back into the kitchen.

"Tawwy."

"Yes, that was your mama. Remember you call her 'Mama' not 'Tawny.'"

"Mama."

"Right. Mama."

"Shit."

I choked on my coffee and spewed it all over the countertop.

"Larissa I told you *not* to say that word. It is a bad, bad word. Ugly."

"Mama shit."

Willow let out a loud, frustrated sigh and covered her face with both her hands. I carried the bowl of cereal over to the table.

"Yes, Mama said that word, but it isn't nice. Pretty little girls don't say that word," Willow began explaining.

Setting the bowl down in front of Larissa, I bent down so I could look her in the eyes. She smiled brightly up at me, obviously enjoying the attention.

"I like princesses, Larissa. Do you?"

She nodded and clapped. "Pinsesses."

Perfect.

"You know princesses don't say that bad word. They like to use the word 'Skittles' instead."

Larissa studied my mouth a moment, as if trying to take that in, and then her big green eyes lifted back up to mine.

"Skiutles."

"Yep, 'Skittles.' It's a princess word."

Larissa beamed and looked at Willow. "Skiutles!" she announced loudly.

Willow laughed and nodded.

"Yep, 'Skittles,'" she replied, looking less tired. Her eyes shifted to meet mine and she mouthed *Thank you*.

I nodded and grinned at her before turning and heading back to the kitchen to make the best damn omelet imaginable.

Chapter Eight

WILLOW

I finished the last bite of my omelet. It had been delicious. I'd been a little embarrassed by how ravenous I seemed after the first bite, but Marcus obviously seemed pleased by my gobbling up the omelet, so I thought, *Screw it*, and enjoyed myself. The boy could cook. Larissa had long since finished her cereal and her chocolate milk. She was currently sitting on the floor with Marcus as he stacked up her blocks just so she could knock them down again. He'd moan and act like it was the worst thing ever that she'd knocked down his blocks, causing her to giggle louder. He was sweet, he could cook, he was good with kids, he was smart, he had goals, he was freaking perfect. No doubt he'd make some country club daughter a very good husband. That thought made me feel like I'd just swallowed a brick.

A knock at the door interrupted my dark thoughts, and I stood up to go get it. Surely Tawny wasn't already here. I wanted her to get groceries first. Larissa needed food.

It wasn't Tawny.

Outside the door stood two girls exactly like the country club member I'd been picturing in my head as Marcus Hardy's wife. Both were blond and dressed in clothes I knew hadn't been purchased at Target or thrift stores. One was by far the more beautiful of the two. She was striking, with long blond curls and blue eyes framed by thick black eyelashes. Lord, please let that be Marcus's sister. She was model perfect.

"Hey, um, Willow, right?" the less intimidating girl said. I forced a smile and nodded. Maybe they were here for Cage. That had to be it.

"Is Marcus here?" My stomach fell.

"Hey, Manda, everything okay?" Marcus said, coming up behind me. Close enough that his chest pressed against my back.

The less intimidating one gave him a sad smile and shrugged. "Yes, as good as they can be."

Crap. The gorgeous one wasn't his sister.

"Can we come in?" Amanda asked when Marcus didn't step back, allowing me to move.

He paused a moment, and I was beginning to get a weird vibe here.

"Uh, well, um, I guess." He stepped back from me, and I

quickly retreated to the floor to take over the job of entertaining Larissa.

"Low, this is my sister, Amanda." He motioned to the girl I'd already figured out was his sister. "Manda, this is Low."

"It's nice to meet you, Low." Amanda gave me a friendly smile, and then her eyes shifted to Larissa and I could see the questions in her eyes.

"And the little princess over there tearing down my blocks is Larissa, Low's niece."

The relief on Amanda's face was obvious. I almost wanted to laugh. She'd been worried I had a kid.

"Low, this is a friend of mine, Sadie." Miss Perfect was the beholder of the musical voice from yesterday morning in the laundry room. Fabulous. "Sadie, this is Low."

Sadie stepped forward and squatted down to smile at me and then Larissa.

"So, you like tearing down blocks too, huh?"

Larissa bobbed her head.

"Well, I've got a little brother at home who has just found the exact same thing entertaining."

Larissa knocked the blocks down and turned back to smile at Sadie as if she understood what the girl had said and wanted to show off.

"You're really good at that," Sadie cooed. The girl was going to be really hard to dislike.

Marcus walked over and sat down on the couch directly behind me. His foot pressed against my hip.

"How's Sam doing these days? Still a pretty boy?"

Sadie laughed, and her voice actually reminded me of soft, tinkling bells. Ugh!

"Sam is a handful, and yes, I'm afraid he's only getting prettier. However, Jax is determined to make him a baseball player. The kid is seven months old and has more autographed baseballs and baseball bats than an actual collector."

Jax . . . Sadie . . . why do those names ring a bell?

"I wouldn't expect anything less with Jax Stone as his future brother-in-law."

My jaw dropped. This was her. The girl. The one who Jax Stone, the hottest rocker in the freaking world, had fallen in love with this summer. Oh. My. God.

"Doesn't mean he has to spoil him," Sadie chimed in reply.

Marcus began playing with my hair, and I forgot all about being starstruck.

I began stacking the blocks again, hoping no one noticed my flushed cheeks from Marcus's attention.

"Mom's fixing lunch and wants us to go eat with her today. She has some things she wants to talk to us about. Sadie brought me here so you and I could ride together. She's on her way to the airport."

Marcus's hand paused a moment, then went back to wrapping strands of my hair around his fingers.

"Yeah, okay."

I chanced a glance over at Amanda, and she was watching Marcus play with my hair with an amused grin on her face.

Marcus cleared his throat. "You picking up or taking off, Sadie?"

I watched as Sadie smiled up at Marcus. He had to be affected by her. That thought bothered me. Even as stupid as that sounded. It did.

"Taking off. Jax is a guest judge on *American Idol* tonight. Then back here tomorrow for a concert in Pensacola."

Holy shizz.

Marcus chuckled and ran a finger down my neck, causing chill bumps to break out on my very bare arms.

"You're acclimating to his life well. See? You had nothing to worry about."

Sadie shrugged, then grinned. "He makes everything worth it."

"*Gag!* Okay, stop with the mushy," Amanda interrupted. Standing up, she motioned to Marcus. "Come on. I need to swing by Dad's and pick up my car. He's just giving me a new one. Figures. Kiss ass."

Marcus's hand froze, and I could feel the tension in his body rolling off him in waves. Something had upset him. Was it his dad giving his sister a car? Or because she called their dad a kiss ass?

Sadie stood up. "I have to go too. I promised Kane, the chauffer driver Jax insist I have, I'd be there ready for takeoff at ten." Her gaze dropped to me. "It was really nice to meet you, Low." I could see the sincerity on her face, and dang if I didn't like her. She flashed her hundred-watt runway smile at Larissa. "And it was wonderful to meet you, too, Larissa. I don't get to meet princesses often."

Larissa clapped happily, at the word "princess," no doubt.

"Good luck, you two," Sadie said, looking from Marcus to Amanda.

"Thanks," Marcus replied in a tense tone as he stood up behind me.

"Thank you for everything. I'll miss you this weekend but I'm going to watch *Idol* tonight, so wave to the camera when it zooms in on you." Amanda pulled Sadie into a hug, and Sadie squeezed her. Something was definitely going on with Marcus's family, and I'd bet money his dad was the cause.

Amanda walked Sadie to the door, then turned back to me. "I loved meeting you, Low. Really, I did. We need to spend some more time together."

I simply nodded, surprised by the other girl's enthusiasm.

"I'm going to walk Sadie out and get my things from the Hummer. I'll meet you in the truck," Amanda told Marcus with a strange expression on her face. It was as if they were having a conversation without words.

"Okay," Marcus replied.

Once the door had shut behind them, I stretched my legs and stood up.

"Martus pay," Larissa demanded.

"No, sweetie, Marcus can't play right now. He needs to go bye-bye."

"Bye-bye too," she demanded, raising her arms up like the Queen of Sheba.

Marcus chuckled, and I could feel the tension in him ease some.

"You make it really hard to leave, princess, but I gotta go. We'll play again. I promise."

Larissa frowned, then nodded as if she was okay with this and went back to her blocks.

"Thanks for breakfast and helping with Larissa," I said, standing up.

"I enjoyed every minute of it."

I felt my face flush again, and I bit my bottom lip to keep from grinning like an idiot.

"Come here, Low," he whispered, reaching out and taking my hand and pulling me to him until my body was pressed up against his. He draped my hand over his shoulder before releasing it to grip my waist.

Marcus Hardy's mouth was on mine before I could take in the fact that I was touching him.

His lips were warm and soft as they played gently against mine. He nibbled my bottom lip and I gasped, opening my mouth just enough for him to slide his tongue inside and begin to leisurely stroke mine. The moan that escaped me was followed by me clinging to him. Both his hands left my waist so they could cup my face while he tilted my mouth and explored it more thoroughly. No one had ever kissed me like this. The minty taste of his toothpaste was the most delicious thing to ever touch my tongue, I swear. His right hand slid down my arm and around my bare back, pulling me up even tighter against him as he continued to nibble and lick every inch of my mouth. His left hand slowly slid down my neck in a gentle caress and stopped right below my collarbone. I whimpered. I couldn't help myself. His big calloused hand was so close to covering my breast. Breaking the kiss, Marcus took a deep breath and moved his hand to my arm while putting some distance between us. I couldn't keep from breathing erratically. I didn't have enough practice with this to keep my reaction under control.

His eyes met mine and we stared at each other. The excitement in his gaze made the fact that I was a complete withering mess a little better.

"Martus tiss," Larissa called out loudly reminding us both where we were and that we weren't alone.

A giggle erupted out of my mouth, and I shifted my eyes from Larissa, who was looking up at Marcus expectantly.

Marcus let out a dramatic sigh, "The ladies, they all want me," he teased, and bent down and kissed Larissa on the top of her platinum curls.

"Bye-bye," Larissa said, apparently pleased with his kiss.

"Bye-bye, princess. I'll see you again soon."

He stood back up and studied me a moment before reaching out and rubbing my bottom lip with his thumb.

"I'm not done here. I'm just beginning, Low. But I couldn't walk away again without that kiss."

My knees felt like Jell-O. How sweet was that? Guys didn't talk to me that way. Marcus Hardy was straight out of those gushy romance novels my mother used to read.

"Okay," was all I could say. Piecing words together right now was impossible.

He dropped his hand, and a sexy smirk touched his lips before he turned and left.

Chapter Nine

MARCUS

"Well, that took a while," Amanda teased as I got into the truck grinning like a fool.

"Yeah, it did."

"She's really pretty."

Pretty did not begin to describe Willow. Seeing her sitting there beside Sadie, I realized how much sexier Willow was. All that copper hair and fair skin and curves. Damn, the girl had curves. Really, really nice curves.

"More like gorgeous," I replied, backing the truck out into the street.

"That's what Sadie said. She was really happy about Low. She seems happy for you. I think she worried you were still pining for her."

I'd stopped pining for Sadie a while back. My attraction to Willow only proved that.

"I mean, I know Cage is a total male whore, but Preston said he was, like, real protective of Low, and then there is that little issue about his claim that he's going to marry her one day."

I gripped the steering wheel tightly, trying to control the violent reaction that reminder caused. There was no way in hell Willow was going to marry Cage. I wasn't ready to propose marriage to her or anything—we were just in the beginning stages of a relationship—but I knew she was better than Cage York. Sure, he was good to her, but he reminded me of a big brother. He treated Willow the way I treated Amanda. Willow deserved so much more in life than that. She was smart, funny, real, so incredibly sexy—she wasn't someone's standby, dammit.

"Your knuckles are turning white," Amanda chirped.

I relaxed my tight grip and took a deep breath.

"Cage is a little confused about things. Low will never marry him. She'll tell you so herself. She's special."

"Like Sadie was special?"

I thought about it a minute, and then nodded. "Yeah, like Sadie, I guess. You don't come across girls like those two often. Trust me, I've looked. They're definitely rare."

"Like I said before, this time you aren't up against a rock star. My money's on you."

I grinned, and reached over and squeezed her knee. "So,

tell me about this car Dad's giving you."

An immediate frown tugged the corners of her mouth down. "My Jeep has all kinds of issues, and Dad said that's what happens when you buy inferior automobiles." She rolled her eyes. "Anyway, he's giving me some trade-in he just got. A sports coupe or something. I think he said a 250CL ... maybe. I don't know. But I need a car and I can't afford one on my own."

Figures, Dad was putting her in a Mercedes. Let the world see that the Mercedes King supplies his daughter with a car. He won't be getting my ass in a damn Mercedes. Nothing was wrong with my Chevy truck. It was paid for, by me.

"It'll be a safe car. If you end up going to Tuscaloosa in the fall, then I'll feel good about you being on the road in a Mercedes coupe."

Amanda fidgeted in her seat and cleared her throat. Uh-oh. That was never good. Those were her nervous tics.

"Um, about college. See, Jamie and Hannah are going to Auburn."

"Ah, *no*! Amanda, please tell me you're joking."

"Let me finish, Marcus, *gah*!"

I did not want to hear this, but I let her continue.

"Like I was saying before you went all 'Roll Tide' monster on me, Jamie and Hannah are going to Auburn. Jamie got a cheerleading scholarship and Hannah's daddy is an Auburn alum, and I want to be a veterinarian. You know I love animals. It's what I really want to do." This was not happening. Amanda shifted in her seat until she was turned toward me. "If you weren't a die-hard Alabama fan and someone asked you the best college in Alabama to go to if you wanted to be a veterinarian, what would you tell them? Hmm?"

I let out a frustrated sigh. "Auburn," I mumbled.

"Bingo! Which is why I applied there . . . and I got accepted."

Well, shit. My baby sister was going to freaking Auburn.

"I mean, I could've applied to an out-of-state college and moved really far away."

I shook my head. "No, I wouldn't want that."

"That's what I thought. I'll secretly still cheer for Bama in the Iron Bowl every year, I promise."

Shaking my head, I decided to focus on that kiss with Low. It made me happy. My sister's choice in college did not.

My dad was standing outside his dealership when we pulled up. He was tall and in shape, with a few silver streaks in his brown hair. He was laughing, all relaxed and happy-looking. You couldn't tell by his jovial appearance that he was tearing his family apart. It didn't appear to be bothering him at all. Clenching my teeth tightly, I kept my thoughts to myself. The last thing Amanda needed was to hear me vent about what a complete ass our father was.

"You getting out?" she asked, glancing back at me as she opened the truck door.

I shook my head. "I'll just see you in a few minutes at the house."

"Okay." The understanding in her eyes reminded me I wasn't alone in this. We were a team.

She stepped out of the truck. My dad began walking my way. I debated spinning off before he could get to my truck window. But for Amanda's sake I didn't. I rolled down the window as he approached.

"Marcus, you're not getting out to see your sister's car?" His question chafed me. As if I didn't care about Amanda.

"I'll see it in a few minutes at my mother's house."

That caught him off guard. He cleared his throat and shifted his feet.

I continued to glare out the front window.

"The other day I wasn't prepared for your verbal attack. I may have said some things I shouldn't have. I apologize. But this is between your mother and me. You kids don't need to be caught in the middle. You're both almost grown."

I jerked my head around and shot my glare directly at him.

"This will always affect me. My mother is falling apart. She's my mama. The woman who fed me soup when I was sick and held me while I threw up. She was the one who fixed my scraped knees and held me while I got stitches because I ripped my arm open. She read me stories until I fell asleep at night. You expect me to just not care that you're hurting her? Hell, you're killing her. My mother and my sister are the only two people in this world I'd die for. I'll do anything I have to in order to make them happy. So *no*, Dad, this isn't just between you and Mom. When Mama cries, Amanda cries. Then I'm the one who has to go pick up the pieces of this mess you've created." I stopped ranting and took a deep breath, because at the moment I really needed to hit something, and my dad's face was looking very appealing.

"I didn't realize your mother was sharing our personal problems with you. I'll speak with her about it."

I jerked the truck door open and stood face-to-face with my father. Our noses were almost touching. My finger was shoved against his chest so hard I knew it had to hurt. "You go near my mother and I will break every bone in your body, old man. Do you understand me?"

My dad's face was bright red. I could see the fury and surprise in his eyes. I'd embarrassed him in front of his employees, and if he said one more word, one of those employees was going to need to call an ambulance for their boss.

Turning away from him, I jumped back into the truck and spun off, leaving tire tracks on his nice paved car lot.

WILLOW

Was it possible that hours later my lips were still tingling from Marcus's kiss? Surely not. It had to be all in my head. I picked up the last spoon Larissa had used to play the drums on the pots and pans. Tawny had finally shown up to get her and had acted like I was being an inconvenience asking her to pick up her daughter. But even my crazy sister couldn't bring me down off my high. The memory of Marcus's kiss and his words had me floating around on a cloud no one could knock me off of.

Yawning, I decided it was time to go take a nap, with all these good thoughts to spur some really nice dreams. Glancing at Cage's bedroom door, I paused. Should I go get in his bed? Did I want to? I turned and looked back at the couch. That's where I wanted to sleep. All my really good Marcus memories were in this room around or on that couch. Surely I'd have Marcus dreams if I slept on it. Grabbing a pillow off Cage's bed and a blanket out of the closet, I headed to the couch for some overdue sleep and hopefully very good dreams.

Warm fingers ran through my hair, then traced the side of my face down to my collarbone, where they teased and caressed the sensitive skin there.

"Hmmm," I murmured, snuggling closer to the warmth holding me. I was having a very good realistic Marcus dream. Strong hands returned to my hair and gently massaged my head. Oh, I liked that. How did Marcus know to do that? Cage always massaged my head. He knew I had a weakness for it. Dang, Cage was messing up my dream. This was supposed to be a "Marcus only" dream. Before I could get too upset, his hand found its way back down to my collarbone. He was driving me crazy. Just slip a hand under my shirt already. Please. I was ready to beg. When his hand started moving north again, I whined, "Marcus, please."

The hand froze. I opened my eyes and stared directly up into Cage's face.

"Did you just call me Marcus?"

Fantastic. What had I done? This was not the way I was going to handle the whole me-and-Marcus possibility with Cage. I rolled my eyes and sat up.

"Probably. I was dreaming, Cage. I can't control what I say when I'm asleep."

Cage scowled. "You were dreaming about Marcus?"

I shrugged.

Cage groaned. "Willow, we talked about this. Baby, he's so not like us. He dates rich babes his parents approve of. He doesn't slum it. Don't set yourself up to get hurt. Please," he pleaded.

If anyone else had referred to dating me as "slumming it," I would have slapped them. But it was Cage, who grew up next door to me. He had lived my life. He was allowed. It was different coming from him.

"Again, it was a dream. I can't control it."

Cage scooted over, closing the distance between us. "You're so dang cute when you sleep," he murmured, leaning over to nip at my shoulder.

"Stop, Cage. Don't start that. If you need to get laid, go elsewhere."

He dropped his head back against the couch. "I just wanted a taste, Low. You're killing me."

I patted his leg. "No, you're just horny and I'm just available."

Cage chuckled. "You think you've got me all figured out, don't ya, love?"

"I know I've got you all figured out. You can't fool me, Cage. I happen to know spiders scare you to death and you cry every time you watch *Extreme Makeover: Home Edition*. There is nothing about you I don't know."

Cage wiggled his eyebrows at me. "You think so?" He leaned over until I could feel his warm breath tickle my ear. Surprisingly, it didn't smell like whiskey . . . yet.

"I beat off to thoughts of you naked and spread out in my bed with that wild red hair of yours covering my pillow."

"*Ugh!* Cage!" I pushed him off me and stood up. "TMI, Cage. I so did not want to know that."

Cage cackled with laughter. "What, baby? You don't think about me when you slip your hands into your panties and get naughty?"

"Cage, SHUT UP!" I screamed, putting my fingers in my ears.

He stuck his pointer finger in his mouth and licked it. I swear, he could be so gross.

"Who do you think about, Low? When you're making it feel good down there?"

I was getting ready to slug the stupid smirk off his face.

"First of all, I don't do *that*. And second of all, you're a pervert. Now go get laid and leave me alone."

Cage sat up and rested his elbows on his knees. His baby-blue eyes were round as saucers.

"You don't stroke it, Low?"

"Oh. My. God. Would you please stop it?!"

Cage shook his head in disbelief.

"You really don't. You've never had an orgasm. I can see it all over your face. Well, shit."

"Cage, I mean it. This conversation—" I stopped as the door opened and Marcus stepped inside. My face went instantly bright red. I didn't have to see it to know it. The idea that he could have heard even a tiny portion of this ridiculous conversation was humiliating.

"Marcus, man, we were just talking about you," Cage said with an evil smirk, and stood up from the couch. I couldn't bring myself to clarify Cage's stupid greeting. Instead, I stood stock-still as Cage walked by me and whispered, "Remember what I said."

I didn't need him reminding me that I wasn't good enough for Marcus. I already knew this. But what he didn't know was that Marcus was completely clueless to this fact. And I wasn't about to point it out to Marcus.

I shoved Cage, and he stumbled and laughed before going into his room and closing the door behind him.

I knew Marcus was waiting on me to say something, but I didn't know what to say. Tucking my hair behind my ear, I glanced over at him.

"Um, hey," I managed to croak out.

A small, sexy smile touched his lips, and I felt like I might melt in a puddle on the ground. If it wasn't for my worry that he'd heard us before opening the door, I would completely be enjoying his smile.

"Did you get some sleep?" he asked, walking over to me slowly with a very determined gleam in his eyes.

I nodded. "Just woke up."

He slipped his hand into my hair and cupped the back of my neck.

"Good," he replied. His eyes drifted down my face stopping to study my mouth before traveling on down to let them drift over my neck and shoulders, then my chest, which was rising and falling pretty darn fast.

"Go out with me tonight, Low. We'll go do anything you want to. We can go eat, dance, walk down the beach, you name it. Just go somewhere with me."

I swallowed hard and bobbed my head up and down.

"Okay," I managed to reply without it sounding like a strangled whisper.

A pleased grin spread across his face, and his eyes locked with mine again.

"We can do all three. I'll take you somewhere to eat. Somewhere nice. Then we can go dancing. I really want to dance with you. Then we can end our night with a walk down the beach."

Oh wow. Yes. Yes. Yes. I nodded again.

"Then let me go get ready, and you do the same. I'll meet you right back here in an hour. Is that enough time?"

"Yes."

Marcus dropped his hand from my neck and stepped back. He gave me one last bone-melting smile before turning to disappear into his room. I fantasized about following him in there. Watching him change. What would his stomach look like completely bare? The tiny peek I'd gotten was mouthwatering. I could only imagine what the rest of him looked like.

"Low, where'd you put my favorite jeans?" Cage broke the spell. I spun around and headed for the closet, where I'd hung up his jeans. Crazy boy couldn't find anything.

I pulled the jeans off the hanger and handed them to Cage. "Right in front of your face," I said, handing them to him.

"Thanks, babe. Look, I got a date. Probably won't be in until late. You stay here. After that crap Tawny pulled on you this morning, I want you here."

I nodded. He jerked his jeans on, and I went back to the closet to find the few things of mine I'd hung up.

"Where you going?" he asked as he tugged on his boots.

"I don't know yet. Out with friends."

It wasn't that I didn't want to tell him about Marcus, because I really did. I wanted to say *Look here, I guess he doesn't think of going out with me as 'slumming it,'* but I didn't. Telling Cage would worry him. Possibly make him get all jealous. I was never sure with him. But I wanted Cage to stay out all night. I didn't want him coming home and ruining my night with Marcus. I kept my mouth shut.

Cage came up behind me and wrapped his arms around my waist. "Be safe. Call me if you need anything! And don't drink too much."

"I'll be sober and home early and safely tucked away in bed," I promised.

Cage smacked a loud kiss on my cheek. "That's my girl." He released me and walked out from the closet. "I'm out. If I don't show up until the morning, don't worry." He started for the door as I walked out of the closet, then stopped. "But call me if you need me."

"I promise you, I'll call if I need you."

He grinned at me, then finally left the room. I glanced

over at the clock. I had forty-five minutes left. I needed to shave and paint my toenails. After throwing a few items to choose from on the bed, I grabbed my toiletry bag and headed to the bathroom.

Chapter Ten

MARCUS

She looked like she'd been dipped in chocolate, and damn if I didn't want a bite. The meal we'd eaten didn't touch the craving Low had ignited in me with the little number she was wearing tonight. I opened the truck door for her to step out, and I didn't stand back. I wanted to lift her down. Letting her body press up against mine while I lowered her was almost good enough to curb my need to touch her. The short, silky sundress hugged her chest, creating some killer cleavage and a tiny waist. Then it flared out at the hips and floated around her until it stopped mid-thigh. All night I'd wondered, if I blew hard enough, would the dress fly up in back?

"Thank you," she whispered, staring up at me as her feet touched the ground. I knew this was the part where I let her go and stepped back, but I didn't like that idea. Instead, I kept my hands on her waist. The tips of my thumbs barely grazed the undersides of her boobs, and damn if the way her eyes widened at the innocent touch didn't make me hot.

"You remind me of those chocolate-covered strawberries we had for dessert," I admitted. Her cheeks turned a pretty rose shade, and a small smile touched her lips.

"How so?"

"Well . . ." I ran my hand up her side, being careful not to touch her breast then traced the low neckline of the dress, barely grazing the smooth skin just above her cleavage. "This dress is the same color as that chocolate, and you look absolutely edible in it."

She caught her bottom lip between her teeth, reminding me of our kiss earlier.

"If I kiss you now, Low, we'll never make it inside. I don't trust myself. And I really want to dance with you," I whispered, taking a step back and moving my hand to her lower back, then steering her toward the entrance. I could feel her erratic breathing against my palm.

I opened the door to the Hurricane Port. I knew Rock and the crew would be here. Jackdown was playing here tonight. I'd debated between keeping Low all to myself and going toward Pensacola to go dancing or bringing her here, where my friends were. I'd decided I wanted them all to know we were out together. I didn't want any question in anyone's mind, especially

Krit's, that she was indeed off-limits. We might not be exclusive yet, but I knew if they all saw her with me that Preston, Krit, and even Dewayne would know to back off. Where Cage's stupid declaration wouldn't scare them off, loyalty to me would.

"Do you want to go sit with everyone, or would you rather get a table by ourselves?" I asked, leaning down to speak in her ear so she could hear me over the noise.

"Doesn't matter to me."

"It doesn't matter to me, either. I intend to keep you on that dance floor wrapped up in my arms most of the evening, so where we sit is pointless."

She turned her head, causing her lips to almost brush against mine. Her warm breath bathed my mouth, and I couldn't stop myself. I slid my lips against hers, licking her bottom lip just the way I'd fantasized about doing when I'd watched her eat the chocolate strawberries. Immediately she opened her mouth to me, and her tongue touched mine cautiously until I groaned and pulled her closer up against me. Her mouth was sweeter than anything I'd ever tasted. Kissing had never been something I thought too much about. But Willow's lips were plump and soft and so damn hot. This time she broke the kiss and took a long, deep breath.

"Wow," she whispered, lifting her eyes from their focus on my thoroughly kissed lips to my eyes. "I want to dance with you, too," she explained, grinning. "That's the only reason I stopped."

Mmmm . . . her dimples were sweet.

Unable to keep the extremely pleased look off my face, I slipped my hand around her back and pulled her against me as we made our way toward the guys. Rock was watching us with an amused grin on his face. He'd obviously not missed our kissing.

"Well, well, well, lookie here. If it ain't my best friend with the lovely Willow," Rock said, tilting his half-full mug of beer at us.

"Damn, man, you about ate her face off back there," Preston teased.

"I just want to be there when someone tells Cage," Dewayne piped up.

"Hello to all of you, too." I shot them all a warning glare. I didn't want Cage's name brought up. "I'd love to stick around and hear some more of your brainless comments, but I'd rather dance with Low."

"Ow, I'm hurt. Injured beyond fucking repair," Preston called out as I turned Willow around and led her to the dance floor.

Pulling her in front of me and cradling her in my arms, I pushed our way through the mass of bodies until we were in the middle of everything and well out of view of the table.

Low turned around, smiling at me when we stopped, and began moving to the music. It took me a minute to join in. The sight of all that red hair cascading over her shoulders as her hips kept beat to the music and the flimsy fabric of her dress glided over her upper thighs made it hard to concentrate. Low wasn't as tightly strung as me. She actually seemed more relaxed than she had all evening. This was her element. She liked to dance. Another thing to file away in my memory. Reaching out, I rested my hand on her hip and pulled her closer. If she was going to move like that, I wanted to reap the benefits of it. She came to me happily, running her hand up my arm as she moved her other arm up and over her head while she rolled her hips. I might not make it very long before hauling her out of here and pressing her up against the nearest empty wall.

WILLOW

I loved dancing. It was freeing and exciting. But with Marcus Hardy's hands on my body it was quite possibly my most favorite thing on earth. I let myself go, and he seemed to enjoy it as much as I did. Sexual foreplay wasn't something I knew much about. But dancing—that I could do. Turning in his arms, I pressed my back against his chest and wrapped my arms around his neck. As my backside moved against him, I felt the brush of his hard-on against my lower back. Oh. This was new. He didn't seem to mind that I could obviously feel it. I kept moving, closing my eyes and laying my head back against his chest. This was going to do wonders for my dreams. His fingers expanded on my waist, and then one slowly slid across my stomach, then back down, moving over to slide down my hip just as it reached my panty line. Okay.

Wow. I could feel my body start to tremble a little. I wasn't sure why, but I liked the way it felt. The second tremble caused Marcus to stop, and his hands gripped my waist hard.

"Low, I need a drink. *Now.*"

I wasn't sure what brought that on, and I didn't want to stop what we were doing. It was amazing. But I nodded and let him lead me back to the table, where only Preston and Dewayne lounged drinking.

"Do you want something?" Marcus asked. His voice sounded a little gruff. I tried to think back to what we had been doing on the dance floor. Had I upset him?

"Coke, please." He nodded and squeezed my waist before leaving me there with Preston and Dewayne.

Feeling deflated, I sank down into the closest empty seat. I'd obviously done something to turn him off of dancing with me.

"So tell me, Low, does Cage know you're out with Marcus?" Preston asked. Frustrated with everyone's need to bring up Cage, I shot him an exasperated glare. "No, and it's none of his business."

Dewayne let out a low whistle. "I bet he'd disagree with you on that one, sweetheart."

Shrugging, I turned away from them and their nosy questions and searched for Marcus. I found Jess first. Then I saw Marcus leaning against the bar talking to her. She was obviously flirting, and Marcus's smile said he enjoyed it. The tense guy who'd left me was gone. He seemed to be relaxed in Jess's company. Suddenly her shoulders slumped and she reached up to wipe at her face. Was she crying? Marcus straightened up, then leaned forward and hugged her to him. I reminded myself that Jess was Rock's cousin and she'd just had a bad breakup. No big deal. Marcus was comforting her. Taking slow breaths, I forced the knot in my stomach to go away. Marcus pulled back, turned his head toward the bar, and said something to the bartender, then took Jess's hand as she led him into the crowd. Away from me. This was not happening. Cage's warning came back to haunt me. I guess Marcus was done slumming it. Cringing at that thought, I stood up.

"You okay?" Preston's voice broke into my thoughts, bringing me back to the table, where I'd been abandoned by my date.

I took a deep breath and nodded, forcing a smile. I wouldn't let them see me cry. No one would know this hurt me. I would not get embarrassed by this. I would not let Marcus Hardy humiliate me. "It's warm in here. I'm going to go get some air," I replied.

"Last time you said that, you disappeared," Dewayne pointed out.

"I'm almost positive that what you saw isn't what it looks like." The concern in Preston's voice was unmistakable.

"It's okay if it is. Just because he came with me doesn't mean he has to leave with me. I've grown up with Cage. I'm used to this behavior." I tried to make my voice sound light and unaffected.

"Marcus is nothing like Cage," Dewayne replied.

I wanted to believe that too, but right now I just wanted to leave. I didn't have a response, so I left.

Only two days later and here I was again. Another bar, alone outside because the same sexy blond bombshell had stolen my guy. Well, technically he wasn't my guy last time, but he had been flirting with me. I stared down at the dress I'd spent twenty minutes ironing because it had been folded up in the bottom of my suitcase for months. There was never any reason to wear it. The guy who'd helped me out of the truck had seemed to really like me. Just me. My eyes started to water and I fought back the sting of tears. I would not do that here. I had my pride. My cell phone was in my purse in Marcus's truck. I hadn't wanted to deal with my phone while dancing. This dress had nowhere to tuck anything. Calling Cage was impossible. Probably a good thing. Last thing I wanted was to have Cage angry with Marcus. We'd barely had a real date.

I reached down to undo the straps around my ankles, then slipped off my heels and crossed the street. If I was walking the two miles back to the apartment barefoot, then I was taking the beach route. Sand was easier on the feet than asphalt. Besides, if tears rolled down my face on the dark beach, no one would see.

Chapter Eleven

MARCUS

"Jess, I don't see them. Like I said, I think you've had too much too drink." Jess crossed her arms strategically under her breasts and pouted. I was beginning to think I'd been had, and that pissed me off. When Jess had come to ask me to help her get to her car out back, I'd told her to find Rock. But she'd said she couldn't find him and there were two big stray dogs outside blocking her path to her car. Leaving Willow with Preston bothered me. She was very worked up from our dancing. So damn worked up I'd needed to put some space between us so I could think straight. When she'd started trembling in my arms as I ran my hands over the tops of her thighs, I thought I was imagining it. But then she did it again harder. By God, no one but me was going to get to witness her orgasm. My heart had almost pounded out of my chest, and I'd been so freaking hard, I was pretty sure I'd have suffered permanent damage if I hadn't gotten her off that dance floor and calmed myself down.

Jess's showing up had been the distraction I needed to lose my boner and catch my breath. Dealing with stray dogs would clear my head. That way I could come back and take Willow on that walk along the beach I'd promised her. I wanted tonight to be special. My flipping that little dress up and sliding my hands between her legs was definitely not what I wanted to happen. Especially considering she had to be pretty damn inexperienced to be brought to an orgasm with just a few touches. Slow, Marcus. I had to take it slow.

"Well, fine, then. I guess you can go back inside to your date," Jess grumbled.

"Yep, I think you're safe," I replied, and headed inside the back door. There had never been any dogs. Of that I was certain. But at least I wasn't sporting the woody from hell anymore. I stopped by the bar and picked up our drinks, then headed for the table. Preston and Dewayne were alone, and the severe looks on their faces made me halt.

Ah, *HELL* no!

I'm an idiot.

Slamming the drinks down on the table, I studied both their faces and I knew. Without asking, I knew.

"When did she leave?" I managed to ask over the sick knot in my stomach.

"Right after you walked off holding hands with Jess," Preston replied.

"Said she was getting air, but we all know that means she's jetting," Dewayne piped up.

"Why did you *not do something*?" I barely contained the roar in my chest.

Preston shrugged, looking somewhat sorrowful. "I did, man. I told her it probably wasn't what it looked like."

"It probably wasn't what it looked like? Really, Preston? That was the best you could do?"

"Hey, don't growl at me. You were the one who was dumb enough to walk off with Jess after almost having sex with Low on the dance floor."

I was going to be sick.

I stalked to the door, wanting desperately to run. Had she called Cage? To save her from me? Opening the door, I stepped into a parking lot full of cars but no people. No Willow.

Why hadn't I told her what I was going to do? Did she not realize I was doing all I could not to find an empty corner and run my hands and tongue all over her body? How could she think I would leave her for someone else? Hadn't I made my interest in her perfectly obvious?

Jerking my truck door open, I climbed in, and my eyes landed on her purse sitting on the seat she'd vacated. Her phone. I reached for the small little red purse that matched her red high heels. Her phone was tucked inside. I pulled it out. One text from Cage.

I'm heading to Destin tonight, baby. Should be back in the morning sometime. Text me when you get home safe.

Dropping her purse, I cranked up the truck and pulled out of the parking lot. She'd had to walk home. In those heels. In the dark. Looking like the damn sexiest thing on the planet. My heart was racing in my chest for other reasons now. Please, God, let her be okay.

Slowly I drove back to the apartment, searching the dark sidewalks for Willow. There was no sign of her when I finally pulled into the apartment parking lot. She couldn't have walked home. She hadn't had time to walk home. Either she was here and someone had given her a ride or—I shook my head. I didn't want to think about the "or." I was already starting to panic. I couldn't think that way. I needed to keep my head. Running up the stairs, I opened the door to a very dark, quiet apartment.

"Willow!"

I ran to Cage's bedroom, but the bed was empty. She wasn't here. I spun around, panicking. Where could she be? I'd lost her. I got one date with her and I'd lost her. I couldn't even take care of her for one night. My head was pounding in sync with my heart. I'd go back and stop people along the way. Maybe someone saw her. Maybe she got a ride with someone and they went somewhere else first. Someone had to have seen something. I ran back to the door, jerked it open, and took the stairs two at time. I'd find her. I had to.

"Marcus?"

I halted and spun around to see Willow walking up the beach with her high heels dangling from her hand. I took off at a run toward her. She was here. She was safe. No one had hurt her. I only had a moment to take in her big expressive green eyes full of surprise before I wrapped her up in my arms.

"You're okay," I declared, needing to let it register with my brain that Willow was okay.

"Yes," she replied in a hesitant voice.

I ran my hand down her hair, needing to feel her. To know she was real and she was here. It took me a second to realize her hands had lodged themselves between our bodies and she was pushing me away. Releasing her, I stepped back.

The sweet face that had been smiling up at me earlier tonight was gone. It was replaced by a very angry scowl. And her face was tear-streaked. Why had she been crying? Oh. I'd forgotten why she'd left in the first place. Jess.

"Low, listen. You don't—"

"No, Marcus. You listen. I realize I may not be the kind of girl you normally take on dates. I don't run in your family's social circle, and, well, let's face it, I don't have a swimsuit-model body. But I have feelings too. Probably much more sensitive than the gorgeous females you normally date. If you want to go off with some other girl, you should at least alert your current date and find her someone to take her home. Don't leave her there to look like a fool. It's not nice!" She pushed past me and started stalking toward the stairs. I stood dumbfounded, watching her.

"Low," I called out, running after her. She stopped and then slowly turned around.

"What?"

"I never would've left you. For anyone. I was an idiot. I made a mistake. I should've told you about the dogs and helping Jess get to her car. But honestly, I was just thinking about the distraction it would be, and I really needed a distraction because you had me so freakin' worked up I could hardly walk."

Taking a deep breath, I waited while she weighed my explanation. I'd keep begging if she needed more. I was not opposed to getting on my knees if it would stop her.

"Dogs?"

I wanted to laugh in relief.

"Yes, dogs. Stray dogs were blocking Jess's path from the door out back to her car. She couldn't find Rock. I wouldn't have gone and helped her if I hadn't needed a little more time before I got near you again."

A small frown puckered her forehead.

"When you say 'worked up'?" She paused.

"I mean *hard as a rock*, Low."

A small smile spread across her face. I didn't wait for her to say anything else. I closed the distance between us and grabbed her face in my hands before crushing my mouth to hers. She made a small little sound of surprise, but then her hands ran up my arms and gripped my shoulders. She was harder to reach standing barefoot. Those heels had helped out a lot earlier. Reaching down, I grabbed her waist and picked her up until she wrapped her legs around my waist. Oh. Yeah.

WILLOW

It dawned on me that Marcus was opening the door just as he backed us up inside the dark apartment. I'd been so lost in his kiss I'd missed the fact that he'd walked up the stairs carrying me. I opened my eyes long enough to see him walk over to the couch and sink down onto it with me straddling him. Pulling back, he stared at me intently.

"We're going to have to stop soon. I'm about at my limit." His voice was raspy.

"Limit?" I asked before raining kisses down the side of his jaw and neck.

"Ah, my limit, Low. You know." He was having trouble talking, and it made me feel powerful. Feeling brave, I flicked my tongue out and quickly licked at his neck. He smelled so good. Moaning, he shifted under me until his erection was pressed against the crotch of my panties. The sensation was too much, and I cried out in shock and pleasure.

"And that's my limit," Marcus said, pushing me off him and standing up. I started to think I'd done something wrong again, but from the way he was breathing like he'd just run a marathon I figured that must be good.

"What's wrong?" I asked, staring up at him, wanting him to just come back down here. I'd found something I really liked.

Marcus closed his eyes tightly and let out a loud groan. "Low, baby, please pull your dress down," he pleaded. Glancing down, I noticed my dress had ridden up around my waist.

"Oops," I said, giggling and pulling it back down.

Marcus let out a small laugh and then met my questioning gaze.

"Low, tonight was amazing. Except for the part where I hurt you and you ran away and scared the bejesus out of me. Being with you is incredible. I want to do it again. Tomorrow. And the next day." I laughed, and he grinned and then continued, "You get the idea. But here's the thing. I don't want to move too fast with you. I'm going to have to work on that, because I'm used to moving pretty fast."

Then why go slow with me? Frowning, I stood up. I barely came to his shoulders when I didn't have the help of heels. I wore heels on all my shoes to give me an added boost.

"I didn't ask you to go slow."

He rubbed his face, ran his hand through his hair, and let out a strange, tight laugh. "I know that, but I want to. You're different. And if I'm right, you're really inexperienced."

Warmth flooded my face. I should have known he'd be able to tell. My kisses can't be what he's used to.

"No, Low, you misunderstood me." He reached out to touch me but stopped himself. "Listen to me. No one, I mean no one, has ever gotten me so worked up with kisses alone. You're perfect. Everything about you is perfect."

Well, that made me feel better. It made me feel powerful. I liked it.

I took a step toward Marcus, and he laughed softly. "Don't tease me, Low," he pleaded.

Sticking my lips out in a pout, I frowned up at him. "Okay fine. I'll leave you alone."

Stepping around him, I headed for Cage's bedroom.

"Low?"

I turned at the sound of his voice. "Yes?"

He looked unsure and nervous. It made me want to go hug him and assure him everything was fine.

"Could you . . . I mean, if I . . ." He paused and took a deep breath. "If I sleep out here on the couch, would you please sleep in my bed?"

I hadn't been expecting that.

"Why?"

"Because I can't sleep knowing you're in Cage's bed."

His simple explanation made me feel tingly all over.

"Okay," I replied, unable to keep the silly smile off my face.

He let out a breath like he'd been holding it. "Thank you."

I grinned and shrugged. "You're welcome."

"But I have to go in there and get my pajamas," I explained.

"Just get all your clothes."

I laughed. "Marcus, you can't just move out onto the couch. That wouldn't be fair. You have a nice, comfortable bed in your room. You shouldn't have to sleep on the couch."

"Then sleep. Just sleep. With me, in my bed. That's what you do with Cage now, right?"

"Yes, but I'm not attracted to Cage."

"We'll work around that. Just please move your things to my room."

As wonderful as that sounded, it also sounded as if we were moving in together. Which was the epitome of moving fast.

"Then we'll be living together? You do realize that's what it would be. That's really moving fast."

Marcus frowned and looked back at the couch.

"You're right. Okay, I'll sleep on the couch for now. Later . . . when we're ready, I'll move into the bed."

"Are you sure about this?" I asked.

"Yes. I want to see where this is going with us, and I can't do that with you sleeping in Cage's bed every night. I want you here. But not in there." He pointed toward Cage's room.

With an explanation like that, how could I tell him no?

Chapter Twelve

MARCUS

I hadn't thought through what I was going to say to Cage. When I'd seen Willow walking toward Cage's room, my insides had clenched. I couldn't let her go crawl up into his bed. Jealousy was ugly, and I had it bad where their relationship was concerned.

Standing at my bedroom door with my morning dose of caffeine, I watched her sleep. She was right in the middle of my queen-size bed curled up in a little ball. All I could see was all that hair spread out on my pillows. It reminded me of flames. I'd always loved to watch fires. And I was pretty damn sure I'd always love to watch Willow sleep. Knowing that when she woke up she'd be warm from my sheets and dressing in my room made the fight I was going to have on my hands as soon as Cage got home worth it.

There was a possibility he'd get so angry he'd kick me out. But then I was banking on Willow threatening to leave with me, and I knew beyond a shadow of a doubt Cage wouldn't let that happen. He might be upset, but he wouldn't lose her. He'd put up with whatever she forced him to put up with in order to keep her close. I didn't get their relationship at all. One minute he reminded me of a pussy-whipped guy around her, and the next he acted like her damn brother. I didn't like it. He wasn't her brother. I wanted him to back off. He didn't cherish how special she was. I did.

Low began to stretch out her legs, and a soft moan drifted from the bed. I watched, fascinated, as she raised her arms up over her head, and finally her face peeked out from under the covers. Her small little manicured hands came down to rub her eyes, and she yawned before finally opening her eyes and meeting my gaze. A slow, sleepy smile spread across her face. I wasn't going to be able to sleep on the couch for long. Of this I was absolutely positive.

"Morning," I said, pushing off from the door frame I'd been propped up against and making my way to the bed. She sat up and leaned back against the headboard.

"Good morning" came her reply, her voice still groggy from sleep.

I sat down on the edge of the bed.

"Sleep well?"

Grinning, she nodded and reached over and took my coffee. I watched as she put the rim to her lips on the cup and took a drink.

"You like it black?" I asked.

She shrugged. "I prefer sugar and cream, but you made it look so good I thought I'd take a sip."

"And was it as good as I made it look?"

She scrunched her nose. "Nope."

Chuckling, I took my cup back. "I'll go make you a cup the way you like it."

I started to get up and her hand grabbed my arm, stopping me.

"Wait, um . . . we need to talk about Cage before he gets here."

I didn't want to talk about Cage. I was going to handle it. Alone.

"I'm going to talk to Cage."

She shook her head. "No, I don't think that's a good idea. I need to get him alone and talk to him. He'll get angry at you and possibly hit you. He won't hurt me. He'll listen to me. I can make him understand."

The idea of Willow and Cage holed up in his bedroom for any length of time bothered me. I wasn't going to let her do this alone. I covered the hand she had on my arm with my free hand.

"Low, I started this. I didn't stay away when Cage warned me to. He's my roommate, and I owe it to him to explain this.

I'll get him to listen to me. And if he throws a punch, I can handle him. Just because I didn't grow up in a difficult neighborhood doesn't mean I don't know how to defend myself."

Nibbling her bottom lip nervously, she reached up and ran her fingers through her tangled, wild mass of hair. She didn't want to argue with me. I could see it in her worried expression. I stood up, then bent over and slipped my finger under her chin tilting her face up to look at me.

"Trust me," I pleaded, then pressed my lips against hers before straightening up and leaving the room. Hopefully, she'd be in the shower when Cage got home. I'd prefer her not to be here when I talked to him.

WILLOW

I desperately needed a shower, but I needed to be dressed and ready when Cage walked in the door. Picking up my phone to check the time, I knew he'd be here soon. Cage wasn't one to hang around the morning after.

Opening my suitcase, I grabbed a pair of shorts and my vintage Guns N' Roses 1987 Banned Rape T-shirt. I had a thing for vintage concert T-shirts. Whenever I came across one at a thrift store, I'd get all giddy. This one wasn't a thrift store find, though. It was one Cage had bought for me off eBay for my birthday last year. I wanted to help ease his anger. I figured my wearing this shirt might help. I quickly brushed my hair, then pulled it to the side and braided it. Until I could wash it, this would have to do.

The moment I opened the bedroom door, I heard the key jiggle in the lock. My nerves hit an all-time high as the door swung open and in sauntered Cage, looking incredibly hungover. His eyes met mine and he started to grin, but the grin fell almost immediately. I was standing in Marcus's doorway. It wasn't a detail Cage had missed.

"Good morning, Cage," I said, forcing a smile. His bloodshot eyes shifted from me and found Marcus walking out of the kitchen with my cup of coffee.

"Morning." Marcus nodded to Cage as he passed him and brought me my coffee. I quickly took it from his hands, for fear Cage might suddenly lunge at Marcus and burn him with my coffee. I kept my eyes on Cage. If he made any sudden moves, I was going to stop him.

"Low, what the *fuck*?"

I cringed at the angry growl in his tone.

Stepping past Marcus, I placed myself in front of him, knowing Cage wouldn't hurt me to get to him.

"Cage, you and I need to talk. Please don't do anything drastic. I'll leave if you force me to."

The hurt that flashed in his blue eyes stung. I didn't like hurting him. Other than Larissa, Cage was the only other person I'd ever loved. Hurting Cage was like hurting myself.

His throat constricted, and his angry glare flashed at Marcus.

"You couldn't stay out of her damn panties, could you, Marcus? I warned you she was mine."

Marcus tensed behind me and started to move, and I followed him. I was not letting him get near Cage without me as a buffer. His hands clasped my shoulders. I waited for him to try to move me, but he didn't.

"I haven't been in her panties, Cage. You know Low better than that. Watch what you say."

Cage took a step toward us, and his fist clenched and unclenched reflexively, his eyes never leaving Marcus.

"You don't fucking *know* her! You're a damn pretty boy with his daddy's money. You'll use her and walk away. She can't handle that. Why couldn't you have just backed the hell off like I warned you?"

Marcus moved me to the side this time.

"You know nothing about me. From the moment I graduated from high school I haven't used one red cent of my father's money. I make my own way. And I would never hurt her. You expect her to sit by and wait on you to stop screwing your way through the damn state of Alabama. That's insane and selfish, Cage. If you care about her at all, you'll let her make her own choices."

Marcus never yelled, but his voice was hard and at times lethal sounding. I set my cup down on the table and prepared to jump between them if Cage made any sudden moves.

"I take care of her. Ask her! I've never let her down. I'm the one who has dried her tears and picked up the pieces when her sorry-ass sister continues to break her heart. Since she was a little girl it has been *me* who has helped her through everything. So don't tell me how to show her I love her. Don't you dare tell me I'm fucking selfish."

Marcus sighed and shook his head. I knew he didn't understand Cage's perspective. But I did.

"I get that you've always been the one there for her. I do. But you have a life, Cage. You go out with girls all the time. Why do you expect Low to just sit and wait on you? Why can't she make her own choices?"

Cage's angry glare finally left Marcus, and his focus shifted to me. The betrayal in his eyes almost undid me. The snarl left his face, and a concerned frown took its place.

"Is this what you want, baby?"

I nodded, feeling the tears fill my eyes.

"Okay. If you want to do this thing with Marcus, then fine. I'll take it and deal with it. But when he hurts you, when he lets you down, I'll be here. My arms are always open for you to run into. I want you happy, and if you think this asshole will make you happy, then fine. You need to live a little too. I can't protect you from everything." His gaze shifted back to Marcus. "But I can be here to hold you when he breaks your heart."

I went to Cage and hugged him tightly. Marcus might not

like it, but I didn't care. Cage was going to accept this. He really would do anything to make me happy.

"Thank you," I whispered in his ear.

His forehead touched my shoulder, and he squeezed me tightly. "If he hurts you, I'll kill him." His words were for my ears only. I didn't doubt him, but I knew Marcus would never hurt me. He was one of the good guys.

"He won't," I assured him.

Cage let out a sigh and kissed my temple. "Yes, baby. He will."

Then he let me go and turned and walked to his bedroom without looking back. Once his door closed, I let out the breath I'd been holding and my shoulders sagged in relief. That wasn't nearly as bad as I'd imagined.

Two warm arms wrapped around me, and I was pressed tightly against Marcus's chest. I smiled to myself while he nuzzled my neck.

"I won't hurt you, Low," he promised.

I nodded. Because I believed him.

Chapter Thirteen

MARCUS

Willow had gone to take a shower. Apparently, she'd put that off afraid I'd face Cage alone. The fact that she'd stood between the two of us to protect me would be funny if it didn't piss me off a little. It made me want to go out and beat the shit out of someone so she could see I wasn't some spoiled rich kid who's never had a busted lip or black eye. She'd met Rock, Dewayne, and Preston. Could she not tell I didn't exactly run around with the country club crowd? I flipped the last pancake and reached to get the butter out of the fridge.

"She moved her stuff. You make her do that?" Cage asked from behind me. Guess we were going to get that private confrontation after all. I pulled out a stick of butter and turned around, closing the door behind me.

"I didn't make her do anything."

Cage snarled and glanced back at my bathroom door. This was the first time she'd showered in my bathroom too. Normally she used Cage's.

"Why Low? You could've had any damn chick in this town. Why'd you have to go and mess with Low?"

When he said stupid shit like that, it made me question his belief she was special.

Setting the butter down, I reached for a knife to slice off some pats to put on our pancakes. Without looking back up at him for fear I'd lose my temper, I responded, "You of all people should know how special she is. Girls like her aren't easy to find. From the moment I opened that door . . ." I stopped slicing and looked up at him. I wanted him to see my face when I told him this. I needed him to believe me. "I knew she was going to get under my skin. Then the more I got to know her, the more I watched her and talked to her, I wanted to get closer to her. And as much as you hate to hear this, she wants to get close to me too."

Cage let out a hard laugh and turned to go back to his bedroom. I went back to slicing the butter.

"I want to believe you won't hurt her. But I know you will. I'm going to stand back and let this play out. Because in the end, she'll come running back to me."

His door slammed behind him.

He was wrong. But I wasn't going to argue with him about

it anymore. As long as he stood back and left us alone, I was good. That was more than I could have hoped for.

I set the table and poured us both more coffee, adding some cream and sugar to Low's. I also placed a glass of orange juice beside her plate of pancakes. I wasn't sure if she liked coffee with her meal. I liked cold milk with my pancakes, so I poured her a glass of that, too.

The door to my bathroom opened, and she stepped out dressed in the clothes she'd had on earlier, but this time her hair hung damp and loose down her back. The ends curled just a little when wet. Her face was scrubbed clean of any makeup, and she was beautiful. Big green eyes taking in the table, then lifting to meet my appreciative gaze.

"Wow. That looks really good."

I pulled out her chair and waved my hand for her to have a seat. Giggling, she made her way over and stopped right in front of me. Standing on her tiptoes, she kissed me softly, then leaned back and whispered, "Thank you."

"You're welcome."

She slid into her seat, and I pushed her chair in, then walked over to my side and sat down.

"I don't think I've ever had a guy pull my chair out and push me to the table before. I always thought it would be kind of awkward, but you made it look as smooth as it appears on television."

I smirked, then reached for the syrup.

"I worked for Jax Stone for a few summers at his vacation house on the island. One of my jobs was serving their food. I pulled his mother's chair out a million times."

Her mouth made a small O shape.

"That's how you know Sadie, then?"

I nodded, and once again I was surprised that my chest didn't ache at the mention of Sadie's name. Damn if that didn't make me smile.

"Um, Marcus," she giggled, and I looked up to see what was so funny. "Why did you give me three drinks?"

This time I laughed and shrugged. "Wasn't sure what you'd want."

Willow bit her bottom lip, still smiling, then reached for the milk.

"With sweet stuff, I like milk."

"I'll remember that."

WILLOW

I had to work tonight, but Tawny had called and asked me to watch Larissa for a couple of hours this afternoon. Marcus hadn't argued with me like Cage would have. He seemed to understand family craziness and gave me a ride over there. He'd made me promise to call him as soon as I was ready to leave. He was going job hunting today, and he had a paper to write for one of his online courses. Leaving him was still hard. I was already addicted to him. Not exactly healthy behavior.

As usual, Tawny was running late. She'd promised I'd have time to go home and change before work, but it looked like I'd be going to work as is. Glancing at my phone for the tenth time, in, like, five minutes, I let out a frustrated growl. Why couldn't she just call or text when she was running late?

The sound of gravel crunching under tires outside ended my frustration, and I went to close Larissa's door so Tawny wouldn't wake her up from her nap. I'd go outside to call Marcus after I'd dealt with Tawny. I didn't want her listening in on our conversation.

Walking by the window, I stopped. Instead of Tawny's piece-of-junk Ford Taurus, there was a very expensive black car in the driveway. That couldn't be good. Turning around, I went to the door expecting a knock when it opened and in walked my sister followed by an older guy. Much older.

"You can go now," Tawny said, sauntering into the house and glancing at me as if I were the hired help.

"Um, okay." I stared back at the strange man. Was this her new sugar daddy? Whoever it was, I was getting an introduction before I left. If Tawny was going to bring strange men around my niece, I wanted to know who they were.

"I'm late and you've got work. Why're you just standing there?"

The man frowned slightly at Tawny and took a step toward me, holding out his hand. "Hello, I'm Jefferson." *That's all I get? One name? What was he freaking Usher? I don't think so.*

"Willow, Tawny's sister," I replied, shaking his hand as firmly as I could. A smile tugged at his lips, and he was instantly familiar. How odd. I'd never met this man before. I studied his face carefully. What was it about him?

"Okay, now you two have met. You can leave." The irritation in Tawny's voice was unmistakable. She didn't want me here. Well, now I was curious. So too bad.

"Are you dating my sister?" I asked, looking back up at Jefferson, the one-named old guy.

"Yes, I am."

"Aren't you old enough to be her father?"

"WILLOW!" Tawny screeched, storming back into the room and grabbing my arm so tightly her nails bit into my flesh.

"What? I have a right to know what and who he is exactly. You're bringing him around *my* niece."

"Get out," she seethed.

I jerked my arm out of her hold and glared at her. "No. Not until I get answers."

"Low, so help me God, I am going to—"

"Lowlow." Larissa's small voice interrupted my sister, and we both turned to see her standing at her door, blond curls sticking up in disarray from her nap.

"Hey, sleepyhead, you're awake," I replied, walking toward her. Little arms raised up in the air for me to pick her up, and I gently lifted her and rested her on my hip.

"Mama," she mumbled in a sleepy voice, pointing to Tawny.

"Yep, Mama is home."

"Dada." she pointed to Jefferson.

My head snapped around and my eyes locked with his. Slowly I took in his nose and eyes. The way his bottom lip was slightly larger than his top one. Could this be him?

Holding Larissa tightly against me, I shifted my questioning gaze to my sister.

She let out a sigh and rolled her eyes.

"Fine. You'll find out soon enough anyway," she hissed. "Jefferson is Larissa's dad. But he's still married and in the process of a divorce. Once it's final, Larissa and I'll be moving out. You can have this place once we're out. I don't ever want to set foot in it again."

She'd broken up a marriage. Larissa was this man's love child. Oh. Shit.

"Close your mouth, Low, and give me Larissa. Then leave, *please*."

I walked toward Tawny in a daze. I'd always wondered if that was the case, but hearing her admit it was like someone had slapped me. Tawny reached for Larissa, and Larissa buried her head in my chest and clung to me.

"No," she said loudly. Tears were in her little voice.

"Give her to me, Low." Tawny was angry.

"Go to Mama now, sweet girl. I have to go to work," I said, gently, easing her small head back to look at me.

"My Lowlow," she announced, wrapping her arms tightly around my neck.

"Yes, your Lowlow, but your Lowlow needs to go to work. Your—" I paused and stared up at Jefferson, ignoring the sick knot in my stomach—"Daddy is here to see you." I felt like I was going to throw up. My sweet baby girl was the product of adultery. It made me want to scream at the top of my lungs. This was so unfair. I hated what Tawny had done, yet I couldn't wish it'd never happened. Holding Larissa in my arms, I could never wish she didn't exist.

"My Lowlow," Larissa repeated, patting my chest. I turned my attention back to her, and she was giving her father a toothless smile while introducing me to him. Tears burned my eyes and I forced them back. Crying would upset her and I needed her to let me leave. Although, running out the door with her wrapped tightly in my arms was tempting. I wanted her away from the truth that would haunt her for the rest of her life. I knew what that stigma felt like. The dad who only visited you when he could get away from his real family. Being the product of an affair. That was me. It had shadowed me my entire life. Not being good enough for my dad to want me all the time. And then the visits had just stopped one day. He'd moved his family away, and I'd never seen or heard from him again.

I had no doubt in my mind Jefferson would do the same thing to Larissa. He'd tell my gullible, stupid sister that he was leaving his wife, but he never would. She'd never leave this house. Larissa would grow up here while one man after another walked in and out of her mother's life. She'd cry herself to sleep for the daddy who'd not wanted her.

"Give her to me and just go," Tawny demanded, ripping Larissa from my arms. She knew what I was thinking. She hated me for it too. The fury flashing in her eyes didn't scare me. The pain she'd eventually face when this man never came through for them and eventually left them alone was what scared me.

"MY LOWLOW!" Larissa howled as her small arms reached for me.

"Shush, Larissa. That's enough," Tawny scolded, only causing Larissa to scream louder.

I wanted to grab her back, but the longer I stood here the worse this would get. Instead, I blew her a kiss, "Love you, my pretty girl." Then taking a page out of Marcus's playbook I said, "Remember, act like a princess. Princesses don't scream." She paused and thought about it a minute while little tears rolled down her face.

"Skiutles," she said frowning.

"Yes, that's right, they say 'Skittles,'" I assured her, then waved good-bye, "I'll see you soon, okay?"

I turned and rushed out the door before the tears came.

I'd walked about a mile when I saw Marcus's truck slow down beside me. He was out of it and over to me immediately. I knew I looked a mess. I hadn't called him because I'd needed to cry and vomit. Walking helped calm me down some and clear my head.

"Low, what's wrong?" he asked, pulling me into his arms. I shook my head and willed myself not to lose it again. I couldn't tell Marcus any of this. My world wasn't something he'd understand. It was ugly. I didn't want the taint that had followed me all my life to be a part of my relationship with him. He'd see me differently if he knew. He'd see Larissa differently. If I wanted us to work, I couldn't share this part of me with him.

"Why didn't you call me? I was writing and glanced at the time and realized you should have called an hour ago. I came as fast as I could." I pulled back from his chest and swallowed the lump in my throat. The acidic taste from puking burned my throat.

"I got in a fight with Tawny. She's an ass. Larissa cried because I was leaving. I hate to leave her like that."

Marcus nodded, and his thumbs caressed my cheeks as he held my face. I really hoped he wouldn't try to kiss me. I needed to brush the vomit from my mouth.

"Family can suck," he agreed. Then he turned and opened the truck door, then lifted me up into the seat.

"Next time, call me. Please," he pleaded.

I nodded and forced a smile.

Chapter Fourteen

MARCUS

I pulled up to my mom's house and parked behind Amanda's new Mercedes. I was a little late, but I'd had a hard time leaving Willow at work after the way I'd found her. Damn, she'd been upset. I hadn't even met this sister, and I really disliked her. If it wasn't for the fact that she was Larissa's mom, I'd hate her. I wanted to tell Willow I knew how screwed up family relationships could be, but dropping my crap on her seemed unfair. Willow was sensitive. She'd only worry over me, and I wanted her happy. Giving her more to stress over wouldn't do either of us any good. Besides, I wasn't alone in this. I had Amanda.

Opening the front door, I walked in without knocking. It was family dinner night. Next week I intended to bring Willow with me. I wanted her to meet my mom. I'd just need to find out her work schedule, and we'd make sure to have family dinner on a night Willow was available.

"Well, it's about time you drug your lovesick tail in here," Amanda teased.

I grinned. No use in denying it. I wasn't in love yet. But I could easily see it going there.

"Lovesick?" Mom asked, stepping out of the kitchen with her stark white apron with the lace stuff around the bottom on, and a glass of white wine in her hand.

"Yes, lovesick. You should see him with her, Mom. He's all sweet and possessive. It's adorable and slightly nauseating."

Mom's face brightened at Amanda's description. She'd been worried about me last summer after the Sadie fiasco.

"And why didn't you bring her tonight? I want to see this nauseating scene myself."

I walked over and hugged my mom because I knew she needed the affection and I was just so glad to see her smile again.

"I will next week. She's working tonight. When I find out her off nights next week, I'll let you know, and we can pick a night she's available."

Mom kissed one cheek and patted my other one.

"Good," she replied, then turned and walked back into the kitchen.

"Cage know yet?" Amanda asked in a low voice as she sidled up beside me.

I nodded and she gasped.

"I moved her out of his room."

Amanda's eyes flew open as wide as they'd go.

"No way!"

"Yep."

"And he didn't kick you out?" She sounded shocked.

"And take Low with me? No. He'd never do that."

"Ah, didn't think about that. Smart move, bro."

I shrugged. "I'm pretty dang brilliant."

"Whatever."

Slapping me on the back of my head, she walked around me and led the way to the kitchen.

Once we had all the food on the table and the three of us were seated, Mom cleared her throat. "Okay, there is something I wanted to tell you both. Since our last little chat, I've made some decisions." The look of apprehension on her face worried me. That couldn't be good. Taking a long swig of my sweet tea, I waited for her to continue.

"I've spoken with your father this week. Several times. I did bring up the possibility of a divorce. I told him that if he wanted out, then fine. I'd let him go." She paused and twisted the napkin in her hands nervously. Also not a good sign.

"He doesn't want a divorce. We both believe he has been going through a midlife crisis." She held up her hand when I opened my mouth, very close to yelling "Bullshit!" at my mother's dinner table. "Don't, Marcus. Let me finish," she pleaded. I couldn't look back at Amanda. This was just going to give her hope. I hated to see the relief on her face. Knowing it would only hurt her even more when Dad screwed up again.

"You haven't been our age or lived our lives. These things happen. A midlife crisis is very common. I understand it even if I don't like it. Your father is letting the girl go. She won't be working with him any longer. He's coming home. We're going to work on mending what has been broken. And I need both of you to stand behind me, us. Having you angry at your father won't help me." She swallowed hard, and I saw the tears glistening in her blue eyes. "I want him to remember how good this family can be together. I want him to want us."

I sat there unable to make eye contact with my sister. I knew she was behind this one hundred percent. I also knew my mom wanted this to work. Dad had given her hope. My getting angry and pointing out the multiple issues with this setup would only upset them. It wouldn't change their minds. Nothing I said would change their minds. They wanted him that much. So I did the only thing I could do.

"Okay, Mama. Whatever you want."

WILLOW

Something had upset Marcus. He'd been his usual attentive, thoughtful self since he'd picked me up, but I could feel his anger under the surface. It had to do with his family. He'd had dinner with them tonight. That much I knew. But I couldn't ask him, not when I wasn't willing to open up to him about my family problems. If he wanted to tell me, he would. My thoughts shifted to Larissa. I stared up at the ceiling knowing sleep probably wouldn't happen for me tonight. As tired as I was, my mind wouldn't shut down.

The door opened slowly, startling me, and I sat up in bed expecting to see Marcus. It was Cage. Frowning, I pulled the sheet up over the T-shirt of Marcus's I was sleeping in. The last thing I needed was for him to have an angry fit in Marcus's bedroom while he was no doubt drunk.

"Cage," I hissed quietly, "wrong room."

He didn't listen to me and closed the door behind him before walking over to the bed and sitting down.

"I'm not that drunk. I know whose room this is."

"Then what're you doing?"

He shrugged and let out a sigh. "I missed you, and going into my empty bedroom and getting into my empty bed sucks."

"Well, you can't sleep in here."

He frowned, and I reached out and squeezed his arm.

"I know. Just wanted to see you. I thought you'd be asleep. I figured if I watched you a little bit, I could go to my room and go to sleep with that image in my head."

He could be so dang sweet. Cage didn't do well with change.

He never had. This was a change that was going to be really hard on him.

"I'm sorry, but he makes me happy, Cage."

His frown deepened.

"Why?"

Why? That list could be endless. But I knew the one answer that would shut Cage down.

"I'm enough for him."

Cage dropped his head into his hands.

"Why am I so screwed up, Low? Why can't I be like him? What the fuck is wrong with me?"

My heart broke a little. Memories of the bruises covering his body and gashes on his forehead and cheek, all gifts from his stepfather, flashed in my mind. He and I both had issues. Mine were just different.

"Our lives haven't been easy," I replied, reaching out to run my hand over his head of silky black hair.

He pulled his hands down enough that I could see his eyes. "But you don't have issues with commitment."

"No, and no one beat me either."

"But you were abandoned. By a man who was too stupid to know what an awesome daughter he had, and even though your mom was there, she wasn't, not really."

Larissa's little face today as she cried because I was leaving her came back to me, and a tear rolled down my face.

"Hey." He reached out and caught my tear. "What's this? I didn't mean to make you cry."

I shook my head and grabbed his wrist. "No, you didn't. It's Larissa." I stopped myself. I needed to tell someone. I needed to talk about this. And Cage knew. He knew what I'd lived through. He'd understand.

"I met her father today."

Cage's eyes opened wider.

"Really?"

"Yep, and he's married and old. Says he's leaving his wife and going to come take Larissa and Tawny away from it all."

Cage didn't ask me what was wrong with this. He didn't have to. He'd held me when I'd found out my father had skipped town with his real family.

"Aw, damn," he whispered.

I nodded.

"Maybe he will, Low. Maybe he won't do to her what your dad did to you."

I shook my head. "No, don't you see? If he leaves his wife, then Tawny has broken up a marriage. Someone else is heartbroken. He'll hurt someone either way. He's married. He's already promised God he'd cherish his wife. Now he has not one, but two families. One of those families will suffer."

Cage blew out a long breath.

We sat in silence for a few minutes. I looked past him

toward the door and thought of Marcus sleeping out on the couch. I didn't want him to catch Cage in here. He still didn't understand the relationship Cage and I had. This would upset him.

"Thanks for listening to me. But . . ." I nodded toward the door, hating to tell him to leave.

He gave me a sad smile and stood up.

"But I need to get out of here before lover boy catches me."

"Something like that," I replied.

He nodded and blew me a kiss before leaving the room.

I lay back down and closed my eyes this time. Saying my fears out loud had helped. Sleep slowly found me.

Fluttery kisses trailed down my face, and I turned to the warmth beside me. When Marcus's clean scent reached my nose, I opened my eyes. He wasn't under the covers with me. That was my first observation. He had on a T-shirt. That was my second observation. His breath smelled minty fresh, and with that observation I tucked my head against his shoulder so he couldn't smell my morning breath.

His chuckle sent shivers through me.

"Why're you hiding?" His fresh breath tickled my ear.

"I haven't brushed my teeth," I mumbled.

He laughed out loud this time.

"I'm sure your morning breath is just as sweet as you are."

"Um, no, trust me, it stinks like the rest of the world's," I assured him, refusing to tilt my face back and look up at him.

"Okay, fine, hide your face from me, but I'll tell you I don't like missing out on your sleepy look."

"My sleepy look?"

"Yes, your sleepy look. When you first open your eyes in the morning, you have the sexiest expression. Your eyelids don't open all the way, and those long eyelashes of yours brush your cheeks and your bottom lip is all swollen from nibbling on it in your sleep."

Wow. Okay, I was completely turned on. And I had stinky breath. Fabulous.

I groaned against his chest. "That just makes me want to flip you over and climb on top of you and kiss you senseless."

"Please, by all means, be my guest. I won't stop you."

Laughing, I slapped his chest and sat up.

"You stay put and let me go do a little morning freshening up. Don't move." I pointed at him to emphasize my demand before sprinting toward the bathroom and brushing my teeth, then my hair.

Running back into the bedroom, I had to stop and sigh from happiness at the sight he made leaning against the headboard. He had on a T-shirt but he was in boxers, and his long tanned legs were crossed at the ankles. And Marcus Hardy's bare feet were downright sexy.

I lifted my gaze back up to his face, and he was smirking.

"Do I meet your approval?"

Laughing, I continued over to the bed, but my earlier threat to jump on top of him seemed a little too extreme. Instead, I curled up beside him and tilted my head up at him this time.

"What? No crawling on top of me and having your wild wicked way with me?" The teasing in his voice made my stomach flutter. Feeling slightly brave now that he'd brought it up, I threw a leg over his lap and straddled him. His smile disappeared and his eyes flashed with interest.

"Let's see, I believe the next step is this," I whispered, taking his face in my hands and then leaning down and kissing him with small, quick pecks all over his lips. Both corners and even the tip of his nose. His hands slid up my outer thighs and underneath my T-shirt to grab my waist. Finding my way back down to his lips, I took a small nip at his bottom lip, then pulled it into my mouth and sucked. A groan erupted from him and immediately he took over. His tongue tangled with mine while we explored each other. He sucked on my tongue, surprising me, and I leaned in closer, pressing down on him.

We gasped at the same time as the heat that had been pooling between my legs made contact with his obvious arousal. As if my body knew what to do on instinct, I rocked against the pressure that was causing wild jolts of pleasure to course through me.

Marcus began breathing hard, and his kissing became more intense. His mouth left mine, and I cried out as he began kissing down my neck and stopping to nibble and lick at sensitive skin along the way. Something was happening inside me that scared me but was so exciting I couldn't stop. I continued rocking, and Marcus's grip on my waist tightened as he pressed me down even closer to the wonderful pressure.

"*Agh*, God, baby." His head fell back against the headboard, and I paused panting and achy but worried I'd hurt him.

"What?" I managed to ask in a strangled whisper.

He opened his eyes, and both his hands left my waist and grabbed my face.

"You. Are. Driving. Me. Crazy." He took short breaths after each word before claiming my mouth again. Marcus slipped a hand down into my panties, and my need to be touched took over. I stopped breathing and looked down just as his fingers slid over my sensitive skin, then met the warmth that was aching so badly.

I sucked in a deep breath just as he slipped a finger inside me. "AH!" I cried out, and squeezed his arms. I felt like I was on the edge of a cliff about to spiral off into oblivion, and I didn't care.

"You feel so good," Marcus whispered in my ear, and kissed down my neck. "So hot. So wet. You're so incredibly sexy." Hearing him praise me as I clawed at his body and made loud, almost pleading noises that I couldn't control made my desperate need worse.

"Please, Marcus," I begged. I wasn't sure what I was begging for, but I was begging. I didn't want him to stop this time. I wouldn't be able to stop. Not now.

"Come for me, Low. I want to feel it." His low voice sounded tight as he spoke close to my ear.

All it took was one small caress just where I needed it, and my world fell apart. It was as if someone had lit a bottle rocket between my legs. The scream I knew was mine sounded like it belonged to someone else as I held on to Marcus, afraid I'd fall if I let go. What had I done? And could I do it again?

When my heart began to slow down and breathing was once again possible, I realized I was wrapped tightly in Marcus's arms and my head was tucked into the curve of his neck and shoulder. Holy. Cow.

I still had a death grip on Marcus's arms, and I slowly peeled my hands away, hoping I hadn't left fingernail cuts on his skin—although I don't see how I could have kept from it.

What had I done? How could I look at him? What was I supposed to say? Did he think I was insane? I was pretty sure I'd just screamed like a banshee. It was a miracle Cage hadn't come bursting in. Marcus stroked my hair as if comforting me.

"Low." His voice was husky.

"Yes," I replied, keeping my face safely buried in his neck.

"Look at me."

Aw, crap. Slowly I pulled back, immediately missing the warmth of my little safe haven.

I lifted my eyes to meet his, and a slow, sexy smile instantly eased my mind. His eyes were hooded as if he'd just woken up.

"What's wrong?" he asked, holding my gaze.

I felt heat rush to my face.

"Um . . . I, uh . . ." What did I say? *I'm sorry for going crazy in your lap?*

"Low." He reached out and ran his hand through my hair, then rested it on my neck.

"Was that your first orgasm?"

Oh.

Well, no freaking wonder. I completely understood the fascination with those things now.

Nodding, I knew my face flushed even brighter. His grin grew to a full one-hundred-watt smile. He was obviously very pleased with this. Well, that was good.

"Did you enjoy it?"

I let out a small burst of laughter. He did not just ask me that.

"I'd say the fact that I completely acted like a crazy person tells you that I did."

He chuckled and leaned forward, kissed me once on the lips, then leaned back. The friction made me gasp. Oh. He was still . . . hard. Weren't they supposed to not be hard anymore once a guy got off? . . . Which meant he hadn't. Oh.

"You, uh . . ." I glanced down, praying he didn't move again, because for some reason I was really sensitive.

"I'm okay. Really, really okay," he said in an amused tone. "I promise."

My gaze went to his arms, and the little red indentions where my nails had bit into him were bright red. I jerked my gaze back to him. "I'm so sorry."

He raised his eyebrows. "Low, those marks are really sexy. What're you sorry for? Trust me, I'll wear them with pride."

Oh.

He cleared his throat, then grabbed my waist and moved me off of him.

"I, uh, need to go get a shower, and if we continue to sit here like this things are going to get a lot more intense," he explained, and leaned over and kissed me one more time before standing up. "I'll be back in a few minutes. We've got somewhere to go today. A friend I'd like you to meet invited us to a thing."

A thing?

I watched as he walked away. His backside was rather impressive. The boxers he had on hung on his hips, and I sighed happily before jumping up to get ready.

Marcus closed the bathroom door behind him. I needed to

get in there and get my makeup bag. I also wanted to get a peek at Marcus in the shower. Naked. I sat back down on the end of the bed and waited until I heard the shower come on. Once I was sure he'd had plenty of time to strip and get inside, I headed for the door.

I turned the doorknob slowly, then barely cracked the door and slipped inside. The shower curtain was plastic, but it was clear. Pressing myself up against the wall so that Marcus wouldn't turn around and notice me, I took in his very bare back. His butt was perfectly round and muscular. The two dimples on his lower back were visible through the plastic curtain. Oh my, this was a nice view.

I'd lifted my gaze to see the rest of him when I noticed he was leaning against the wall with the support of one hand. His other hand was . . . Oh wow.

A soft groan escaped him as his shoulders bent forward a little. "Ah, yeah, baby. That's it," he whispered. I took a step forward, wanting to hear more.

The muscles in his back bunched as his arm moved in front of him. "So hot, Low. So fucking hot."

I froze. My heart started slamming against my chest. He was thinking about me as he . . . masturbated? I should leave him alone, but I couldn't. I wanted to watch him. It was the sexiest thing I'd ever seen.

"Uh, oh, God, yes," he groaned as his arm began pumping

faster. I reached down and grabbed the edge of the sink to keep from sinking to the floor. My knees were going a little weak.

"Fuck, baby," he moaned, and his body leaned in farther toward the wall. He was close. Did I want him to catch me? Probably not a good idea. But I wanted to hear him and watch his body as he got off. I'd never seen a guy come before. And watching Marcus would be amazing.

His panting got louder and his murmuring increased. I forced myself to back up until I was able to slip out the door without a sound.

Chapter Fifteen

MARCUS

Watching Low step out of the bathroom dressed in a red sundress that stopped right above her knee with a pair of cowboy boots on caused me to momentarily forget to breathe. The image of her in my lap, her eyes glazed over with pleasure as she cried out my name was going to make it so hard to move slowly. I deserved some sort of award. Getting myself off in the shower had only given me a little relief. I could've so easily made love to her. She'd have let me. Wait. Did I just say "love"? . . . When had I ever thought of it as making love? It was sex. It'd always been sex. Sometimes really good sex. But just sex. My eyes traveled up to her face. Her hair was parted down the middle and clasped in two low pigtails draped over each shoulder. Who the hell knew pigtails could be so sexy? Finding her eyes watching me warily, I smiled. She was mine.

"Is this okay?"

I swallowed the lump in my throat. Ah *hell*, when did I go and fall in love with her?

"Yeah, you look amazing."

She beamed at me, and I walked over to her and took her hand in mine.

"Where are we going, exactly?"

I wanted to surprise her, but looking down at her, I fought the urge to take her back to my bedroom and lock her in there with me. I'd be able to keep her forever that way.

"You don't by chance have a thing for rock stars, do you?"

She frowned and shook her head slowly.

"No, why?"

I felt a little better, but the need to keep her safely tucked away still tugged at me.

"Okay, good. No reason. Come on, let's go do this."

She laughed and followed me.

The place was packed. Not exactly surprising. I pulled up to the security gate. A guard stepped out of his station and approached my truck. I rolled down my window and waited.

"Can I help you?" he asked, frowning down at me.

"Marcus Hardy and guest. My name's on the list."

The guard nodded and spoke into his headset, "Got a Marcus Hardy and guest."

"Let me see some ID," the guard said, somewhat more friendly. I pulled my wallet out of my back pocket and handed it to him. He checked it out and handed it back.

"All right, Mr. Hardy, when the gate opens, take the road around to the right. Park over in the small parking lot. Then the second entrance door will have another guard. He'll need to see ID again before he lets you inside."

"Got it, thanks."

He nodded and stepped back as the gate opened. I started to pull through and glanced over at Willow. She was taking everything in. Her eyes met mine and she grinned.

"We're about to go backstage for the Jax Stone concert, aren't we?"

I laughed. I guess that was an easy one to guess after all that security stuff in order to enter a private entrance to a civic center crawling with people.

"Lucky guess," I replied.

She clapped her hands together once and squealed.

"Oh, wow! I've never been to a concert before, and my first one I get to go backstage."

I pulled into an empty parking spot and turned off the truck before looking at her.

"You have all kinds of vintage rock concert T-shirts," I pointed out.

She shrugged. "I like them. I figured I'd never actually go

to a real concert, so I buy them whenever I find one at a thrift store."

Interesting. I filed that piece of information away for later.

"So your excitement is because it's a rock concert, not because you're about to meet Jax Stone?" I needed to clarify this for my own peace of mind.

She giggled, then raised her eyebrows teasingly, "Wel-l-l-l-l, that is kind of cool. I've never met anyone famous before."

Why was I jealous? This was stupid. Jax loved Sadie. He wasn't going to swoop down and take Low from me. I nodded.

"Okay, fair enough."

I went around and got Willow out of the truck, and then we headed for the door. The security guy checked us both out this time. He actually checked Willow out a little too much for my taste. I should have made her change. That getup she had on was damn distracting.

As soon as the door opened, Sadie greeted us.

"You made it." She beamed at me, then Willow.

"Yep," I replied, smiling at the excitement in Willow's eyes as she took in everything around her.

"I'm so glad. Follow me. I want Jax to meet Willow before he goes out. He's had a little girl and her mother in there the past thirty minutes. It's a long story, but we met her at Sea Breeze Foods this summer, and she recognized him even though he was incognito. He gave her his personal card and a promise to get her backstage passes for his concert here. Then he ended up canceling that concert due to some things with me and my family. Anyway, this is his makeup concert, and he wanted to make it extra special for her since she has had to wait so long."

"How sweet," Low said, a little too dreamily for my taste. *Shut up, Sadie.*

Tightening her grip on my hand, Willow glanced up at me, and her excited expression squelched my moment of jealousy.

"Here we are," Sadie said, and patted the bodyguard moving out of our way on the arm.

"Thanks, Ryan," she said, and the angry giant actually grinned a little, then went back to scowling.

"I'm back and I have company," Sadie said, walking into the massive room that reminded me of a hotel suite. Jax stood up from the large black leather chair he'd been lounging in and flashed his rock-star smile at Willow, and I hated him all over again. Why the hell had I brought her here?

"Marcus." He nodded in greeting.

"Jax," I replied, trying real hard not to sound annoyed.

"And you must be Willow. I've heard quite a bit about you the past forty-eight hours."

Sadie had been talking to Jax about Willow. Things started to fall together as to why we were here. Sadie wanted to show Jax that I'd moved on. I wasn't pining away for her.

I had to admit I liked that.

"Oh, w-wow. Um . . ." Willow stammered. Jax made her nervous, and suddenly I was annoyed again.

"He has that effect on people," Sadie joked, and walked over toward him. He wrapped his arm around her, pulling her against him, and kissed the top of her head. That made me feel better.

"I can imagine," Willow replied, tightening her grip on my hand. She was nervous. I wanted to fix it, but I wasn't sure how to help her relax.

"So, Willow, do you like my music, or did you come because Marcus made you?" Jax asked, a teasing tone to his voice.

"Oh, I like it. I actually didn't know where we were going. He was vague." She glanced up at me, smiling. "But I figured it out when we came through security."

Jax found that amusing.

"Well, that's a relief. Sadie hated my music when I met her. I'm a little gunshy with southern girls now."

"Jax Stone, your ego is just fine," Sadie chided, and walked over to the bar.

"Come have a seat, Willow. I'll fix us something to drink. Why don't you show Marcus around backstage, Jax?"

Jax raised his eyebrows at me. He knew as well as I did that this was Sadie's way of mending fences between Jax and me. I turned my attention to Willow, whose death grip on my hand had eased up. "You okay with that? I'll stay with you if you want,"

I whispered in her ear in case she wanted me to stay.

She nodded, and kissed my cheek. "I'm fine. Sadie doesn't make me nervous."

Figures. Stupid rock god.

I squeezed her hand and laid a kiss on her mouth before looking back up at a very pleased Jax.

"You ready?" he asked.

I nodded and followed him out the door.

The moment we walked out the door, another bodyguard appeared and walked behind us. I was used to this. I'd worked for the guy long enough.

"This is where we shake hands and call a truce, I believe," Jax said opening a door, and leading me into a large room, where band members were all lounging around with drinks, laughing and talking to girls draped all over them.

"I guess so."

A girl walked up to us with two bottled waters on a tray. Jax took both of them, handing one to me.

"I'll get you something stronger if you want. I just don't drink before a concert, or much at all. Sadie isn't crazy about it."

"Naw, this is good."

"You don't even notice Sadie anymore. I like that."

I chuckled. I imagined he did. "I bet."

Jax grinned and took a long swig of water. "You in love yet?"

I thought about his question and this morning. "Yeah, I

think I might be. Kind of happened fast. But she's hard to resist."

"Been there, man, and I can honestly tell you that I completely understand."

I guessed he could. Weird. He wasn't all that bad.

"Sadie's really happy for you. She's talked nonstop about Willow since she met her. I know all about how sweet you are with her and how you look at her like no one else is in the room. All kinds of sappy crap."

That made me laugh. "I can't imagine it bothered you too much. If I'm all sappy with another girl, then your girl is safe."

Jax smirked. "I'm the one she loves. I wasn't worried."

He was right. Besides, I didn't care. Not anymore.

WILLOW

My ears were ringing when we left the concert. But it didn't diminish my excitement. I had my first concert T-shirt that I'd actually earned clutched tightly in my hand as Marcus lifted me into the truck. I watched him as he made his way around the front of the truck to get inside.

"Well, what did ya think?"

"I loved it! Thank you for bringing me."

He leaned over and kissed me hungrily, which I hadn't been expecting. When he finished, he nipped at my bottom lip, then released me. I was a little breathless.

"I've been wanting to do that for the past two hours," he

explained with a sexy grin before cranking up the truck.

Wow. Today couldn't get any better.

I lay my head back and rested my eyes.

"Wake up, sleeping beauty, we're home," Marcus whispered in my ear, jolting me awake.

I'd slept the whole way back. Dang it. I'd wanted to spend time talking to Marcus. We'd been unable to do much talking today.

"I'm sorry I feel asleep."

"Don't be. I got to watch you sleep for over an hour. I liked it."

He always made me feel so special.

"Okay, but that sounds boring."

He gently bit my earlobe, then whispered, "Trust me, it wasn't."

I shivered and his breath hitched.

"Let's go on inside." His voice sounded tense.

I quickly scrambled out of the truck. If we were going to continue this inside, I was more than willing.

Marcus walked around and grabbed my hand, pulling me up beside him as we made our way up to the apartment.

Once inside I headed over to the fridge to get a Jarritos. I was thirsty. Opening the bottom drawer, I realized there weren't any more. Only beer. Cage never ran out of my drinks. But they were gone. He was letting me go. A small bubble of fear welled up inside me. I closed the fridge and stared blankly at the stainless steel in front of me. What if he moved on and left me? What would happen when Marcus left me? I'd be alone. Cage was my safe haven. My heart started racing, and I looked toward his bedroom door, panicked. Where was he? He hadn't texted me all day to tell me what he was doing or to check on me.

"Low, you okay?" Marcus asked. I wanted to nod but I couldn't. The panic in my chest was starting to take over. It had been a long time since I'd had an anxiety attack, but I was about to have a full-blown one right here, and there wasn't a thing I could do to stop it. Cage hadn't remembered my Jarritos. He was letting me go. I'd asked him to and he was doing it. Marcus wouldn't be around forever.

"Low, look at me." Marcus turned me around to face him, but I couldn't meet his eyes. I'd lose it. Deep breaths. I had to focus on taking deep breaths.

"Low, look at me, please, baby, look at me," he pleaded, and I wanted to ease his concern but I couldn't. Right now I had to breathe. In and out, in and out, in and out.

"What the hell, Low." Cage's voice. "Move," he barked, and I wanted to stop him but he was leaving me. "Low, snap out of it. Come on. Snap out of it for me. Focus on me, Low, and tell me what happened." Cage's voice was stern. He'd been with me through these before. He'd stop it. I turned my eyes up to him.

"Jarritos," I choked out, and tears stung my eyes. Gasping for air, I focused on my breathing again.

"Ah, shit, Low. I got some more. See, they're right here in this bag."

I saw the familiar bottles through the plastic bag. He'd bought some. He wasn't leaving. I was safe. I wasn't alone. Nodding, I took a deep breath.

"'Kay," I replied in a whisper. The tightness in my chest eased some, but I could feel the threat of an attack still there. Waiting on me.

"Come here." Cage pulled me against him, and the familiar smell calmed me. "I noticed they were gone this morning. I'm not leaving you. Do you hear me? I. Am. Not. Leaving. You."

Nodding against his chest, I heard a door close. Marcus. Oh, God. He'd seen me lose it. Now I was all wrapped up in Cage's arms. Not good. Pulling back, I looked over Cage's shoulder, and Marcus was gone.

"He left," I whispered, lifting my eyes up to meet Cage's.

"You probably scared the shit out of him. It isn't easy to see you do that."

I nodded.

"It was because I didn't have your drinks?"

I teared up again and shrugged. "Sorta. The idea you were letting me go and I'd be alone."

He shook his head. "Never gonna happen. If the damn

Mexican drinks run out and I'm a little slow getting some more, it doesn't mean I'm letting you go. You'll never be alone, Low. I swear to you. You hear me?"

"Yeah."

He glanced back over his shoulder.

"He didn't leave the apartment. He went to his bedroom."

"Thanks." I reached up and hugged him, dreading the idea of facing Marcus.

"I love you, Low," he whispered.

"I love you, too," I replied, and stepped back. I had to go deal with Marcus witnessing my craziness. Cage couldn't do that for me. It was all me.

Chapter Sixteen

MARCUS

I sat on the edge of the bed and cradled my head in my hands. What the hell had just happened? And why had I not been able to reach her? Watching her bury herself in Cage's arms had been more than I could handle. The jealousy that he was the one she went to ate me alive. I was second best. Again. But this time it was ripping me apart. Sadie hadn't consumed me this way. She hadn't owned me. Low did.

The door opened slowly, and I turned my head to see Willow stepping inside the room. I watched as she closed the door behind her. The worry and fear in her eyes killed me, but I didn't go to her. She hadn't wanted me. It had been Cage she'd wanted.

"I'm sorry you saw me like that," she said in a small voice.

That was why she was sorry?

"You turned to him. Not me."

Her eyes widened in surprise.

"I was having an anxiety attack. I was focused on breathing. When I heard Cage's voice, I knew he'd help me through it. He's had to help me through a lot of them."

"I could have helped you."

Her eyes glistened with unshed tears, and she took a tentative step toward me, then stopped.

"I needed Cage because the attack had to do with Cage. I needed reassurance from him."

What?

"I don't understand," I said, sitting up and watching her take another step in my direction.

"You see, Cage has never left me. My father left me. My mother left me. My sister left me. Cage never left me. When people would leave me, he was always there. He is the one person I've always depended on. I've always known that no matter what he'll be there." She stopped and took a deep breath. "When I opened the fridge and my drinks were gone, well, that's never happened. I thought he was letting me go. I thought he was leaving me too."

Ah, damn.

Standing up I closed the distance she'd been afraid to bridge.

"I'm here. You have me."

She gave me a sad smile.

"One day, whatever this is will end. Relationships always do. Then you'll leave me too."

She'd been hurt so much.

I took her face in my hands and held her gaze.

"Listen to me. I'm in love with you. Mad crazy in love with you. I'm not going anywhere. Ever. You can't get rid of me."

A tear rolled down her face, and I swiped it with my thumb, then kissed the tip of her nose.

"I really want to believe you, and I think you really believe that, but Marcus ,where I come from, people leave."

If it took me the rest of my life, I'd prove to her I wasn't going anywhere. She just needed actions, not words. Words she'd heard before.

"I'll spend the rest of my life proving it to you."

She closed her eyes. "I hope so," she whispered.

I reached down, grabbed her hand, and pulled her over to the bed. I'd come up here thinking about doing a little more of what we'd done this morning, but things had changed. Now I just wanted to be the one who held her. I wanted to make it all better. Just me.

I opened my eyes and I was alone in bed. Sitting up, I ran my hands through my hair, then stood up to go find Willow. When I opened the bedroom door, Larissa smiled up at me. "Martus," she announced loudly.

"Princess," I replied, smiling down at her. Two little arms lifted in the air, and I reached down to pick her up. I'd already learned that wordless demand. "I didn't know you were coming to visit me."

She clapped. "Martus pay."

"He just woke up, Larissa. Give him a minute," Willow chided her as she walked out of the kitchen.

"I made some chicken fettuccini alfredo, if you want some. Tawny stopped by unexpectedly about an hour ago and dropped Larissa off. I'm supposed to work tonight, but if I didn't keep her she was going to leave her with this awful lady down the street all night long. I couldn't let her do that, so . . ." She shrugged.

"I'll keep her."

Willow froze and stared at me.

"You will?" The shock on her face hurt a little.

"Yeah, of course. I was going to stay here tonight anyway. She and I will build blocks and knock them over, play with spoons—we'll have a blast."

A smile broke across Willow's face that made me feel ten feet tall.

"Okay, um, thanks, I mean, wow, are you sure?"

I walked over to her and leaned over to place a quick kiss on her surprised little mouth.

"Very sure."

"Martus tiss," Larissa said happily, then leaned over and laid a very wet kiss on my cheek.

Willow giggled. "All right, you. Don't go stealing my man."

Her man. I liked that a lot. A whole damn lot.

"Impossible. Even for adorable curly headed blondes," I assured her, and ruffled Larissa's hair.

"Martus pay," Larissa announced again.

"Yeah, I heard you, chick. Let's go play," I replied.

"Wait, aren't you hungry?"

I'd forgot she'd cooked. My stomach rumbled and I looked at Larissa.

"Can I eat first, then we'll play? You can sit beside me and eat too."

"Bite bites," Larissa responded.

As I turned to Willow for a translation, Larissa proceeded to chant, "Martus bite bites."

"'Bite bites' is what she likes to call eating," Willow explained.

"Makes complete sense to me," I replied, and both girls giggled.

WILLOW

The television illuminated the dark apartment when I stepped inside. There was no sound coming from the TV, but the *Tonight Show* was on the screen. When my eyes adjusted, I found Marcus sound asleep on the couch with Larissa snuggled up on his chest also sound asleep. Blocks were scattered across the floor, and what looked like cookie crumbs made a trail from the living room to the kitchen. My heart swelled. I loved him. I never thought this would happen. I never expected to love anyone else. Not this way. I picked up the blocks and stacked them back in the basket I kept here for when Larissa came over. Then I leaned down to whisper in Marcus's ear, "I'm home."

His eyes blinked open, and then a sleepy smile greeted me.

"Hey," he mumbled.

"I'm just going to take her and put her in bed with me. I'll get you a blanket and pillow."

"I can take her," he said, starting to sit up. I placed my hand on his shoulder and pushed him back down.

"No, you stay put. I'll do it." I kissed the small frown between his eyebrows and took Larissa from his arms.

After tucking her in and securing her with pillows, I went back out to the couch with a pillow and blanket for Marcus. He hadn't moved. He was exhausted, no doubt. Keeping Larissa wasn't for the fainthearted. His eyes were closed. Long blond eyelashes brushed his cheekbones. I bent over him to put the pillow under his head, and two hands grabbed my waist and pulled me down on top of him.

"Mmmm, that's better," he whispered before claiming my mouth. His mouth was sweet and gentle at first, but the more I shifted my body the more aggressive the kiss became. The warmth of his mouth tasted like chocolate chip cookies, and I couldn't get enough of him. I grasped the front of his shirt, pulling him closer. His hands moved up my thighs and cupped my bottom. He squeezed and moaned as I pressed against him. We were going there again. Before we went any further, I pulled back and looked down at him. The desire in his eyes undid me.

"I love you, too," I whispered.

His eyes widened, and then his mouth was back on mine. This time wide awake and determined. I wanted all of him. There was no question in my mind. His hands were everywhere, and I felt shaky all over from excitement. Breaking the kiss, he started tugging on my shorts.

"Take these off," he demanded.

I stood up, nervous but so incredibly excited I couldn't keep from trembling. I wasn't sure if he wanted everything off. Raising my eyes, I looked at him, and he shook his head.

"Keep your panties on. I don't want our first time to be on this couch, and if you take those off I'm a goner."

Smiling, I straddled him and eased down until I felt the hardness I'd craved pressing against me. The image of him in the shower and the naughty things I'd heard him saying replayed in my head.

"I want to take off my panties," I admitted, gazing down at him.

Marcus's heavy-lidded eyes opened wider, and he shook his head.

Swallowing, I leaned over him and lowered my mouth to his ear. "But I know you want to too. I saw you in the shower. I heard you. I want that. What you were imagining. I want that."

Marcus took a ragged breath. "God, baby, you're going to kill me. I'm trying to be good here."

I didn't want him to be good. I wanted him to talk to me the way he'd talked to me in the shower. The way he obviously wanted to. "I know you want more."

Marcus reached up and ran his hand through my hair, then cupped my head. "Yes, I want more. So much more. But I need you to let me go slow. As much as I want you, I need to make sure that when we look back one day and remember how it all happened, I want you to feel cherished. Special. That's important to me."

My insides melted a little, and I bent my head and kissed his lips. I'd let him choose the pace. If he was going to say sweet things like that, I'd let him decide anything he wanted to.

"Then can I touch you? The way you touched me?"

Marcus's body stilled and he stared up at me. I could see the desire in his eyes. I could also see his internal battle. He wasn't sure he should let me do that.

I slid back down his body and found the button to his shorts. I quickly undid it and slipped my hand inside before he could think too hard about what I was doing. I rubbed his erection through the boxer briefs he was wearing, and he let out a sharp hiss. That was all the encouragement I needed. I tugged his shorts and underwear down until I could wrap my hands around him.

"Low, *holy shit*. Baby, what are you doing?"

I flashed him a wicked smile before I began sliding my fist up and down his hard length. "I want to touch you too. It isn't fair that you had to go to the shower and do this yourself."

Marcus closed his eyes tightly and laid his head back. "*Agh!* God. I don't know how long I'm gonna be able to let you do this. *Fuck*, Low, your hands feel good."

I felt powerful. I was making him feel good this time, and I loved it. I tightened my grip and pumped harder. "Does that hurt?"

"*Jesus,*" he breathed, opening his eyes to look down at me. "It feels fantastic."

His obvious pleasure was making me brave. I lowered my head and placed a kiss on the tip. Marcus's hips bucked underneath me and a stream of curse words followed. Both his hands grabbed my head. "Baby, don't go there."

Grinning, I stuck out my tongue and took a lick, causing him to tremble underneath me. I'd never even touched a guy like this before, much less kissed or tasted him this way. But seeing the ecstasy on Marcus's face had me wanting to do so much more.

Opening my mouth, I slid down over it until I had to stop. The hands touching my head were now tangled in my hair.

"Oh, God, baby. Shit. This is fucking heaven." Marcus moaned as I began moving my mouth up and down his shaft.

His panting and murmuring got heavier and more intense. "That's so good. Your mouth is perfect," he encouraged me, making me force it in farther each time. I was just getting the hang of it when Marcus pulled me away from him.

"Stop, I'm gonna come," he said, holding me back as he shivered underneath me.

He covered himself with one hand as he sucked in a hard breath.

"Do you need something?" I finally asked, after snapping myself out of the fascinated haze I was in watching him get off.

He chuckled. "Yeah. A shower."

Smiling, I crawled off him and stood up. "Go get clean," I replied.

Marcus swung his legs over the side and pulled his shorts up some before standing up too. "You are amazing," he said with an awed reverence.

"So are you," I replied.

He winked. "Then be naked, except for those panties, right here when I get out. I'm not done with you just yet."

Chapter Seventeen

MARCUS

I'd just had the absolute best week of my life, and now I had to end it with a family dinner. One where my father would be present. I wished I hadn't promised my mom I'd bring Willow. This was the last thing I wanted her to witness. Willow came up behind me, wrapped her arms around my shoulders, and leaned down to kiss my cheek.

"Almost done with that paper?" she asked, standing up and walking around the table to sit across from me. My University of Alabama T-shirt looked good on her. She no longer wore Cage's shirts around the apartment. I wanted her in mine. Maybe it was a little caveman, but I didn't care. And neither did she. I was almost positive she liked it.

"Almost, but I could use a distraction," I replied.

She smirked and shook her head.

"Nope. I've distracted you all week. You need to finish."

"Please," I begged, and she giggled.

"I'm going to get ready to meet the folks, and you need to finish that paper. We can work out your reward for a job well done later."

I loved how relaxed she'd gotten with me. Her teasing was so incredibly sweet.

"And there's the distraction I need right there. You've given my fantasies some fuel."

Laughing, she closed the bathroom door behind her.

Shaking my head to clear the images of Willow straddling me and crying out my name, I studied the screen in front of me again. She was right. I needed to finish this. Like, yesterday. But I'd spent every spare minute I had with Willow, and I wouldn't have had it any other way.

The apartment door opened and in walked Cage, followed by Preston. They'd been at baseball practice. Both of them were dirty and sweaty.

"Marcus, what up," Preston called out as he came inside and made his way into the kitchen behind Cage.

"Writing a paper," I grumbled, knowing I wasn't going to get anything done with these two here.

"I pay smart chicks to do those for me," he bragged and I rolled my eyes. He'd been "paying" smart chicks to do his homework since middle school. However, his paying normally didn't involve cash.

"Where's Low?" Cage asked before taking a swig of beer.

"Getting a shower. She's going with me to meet my family tonight."

Preston let out a whistle. "The family. That's serious shit right there."

Cage grunted his displeasure and took another drink of beer.

Preston's eyes shifted between the two of us. I could see the curious questions in his eyes. How were we getting along? Did we ever fight? Wasn't it uncomfortable? And the truth was no. Cage was rarely here.

The shower cut off, and I jumped up. Both guys stared at me like I was crazy. The idea of Low walking out in her towel thinking it was just me here scared the shit out of me. I ignored them and made my way to the door.

"Low."

"Yes."

"Preston and Cage are out here."

"Okay, um, could you bring me my things? They're on the bed." That's what I'd been afraid of.

"Yep."

I didn't look back at either of them, but I could feel their eyes boring into me. No doubt Preston was amused and Cage was pissed off.

A pair of pink silk panties that consisted of very little mate-riel and a matching bra lay on top of that brown sundress that reminded me of chocolate. Picking them all up, I headed back to the bathroom, making sure to keep her underclothes hidden from prying eyes.

I knocked. "Got them."

She cracked the door and reached out and took them from my hands, smiling bashfully up at me. I wanted to push my way inside but kept my cool.

She closed the door, and I turned around to face the firing squad.

Preston started up first. "A little possessive there, aren't ya, bud? Afraid I'm gonna get a peek at Miss Low in her towel?"

I shot him a warning glare and sat back down.

"I've seen her in a bath towel many, many times," Cage said smugly.

Taking a deep breath, I forced myself to remain calm.

"The difference is, she's mine now."

"No, she's just yours for now," he replied.

I turned and glared at him. He was leaning against the counter looking so damn sure of himself.

"Forever," I corrected him.

Cage shoved off from the counter and raised his eyebrows. "We'll see."

I started to stand up, and Preston grabbed my arm as Cage walked into his bedroom.

"Don't. Just let it go."

I sat back down. Not because Preston had told me to. But because Low would want me to.

"He's a jerk. Always has been. Just ignore him."

Easier said than done. "She's mine," I repeated, mostly for myself than anyone else.

"Got it, bro. She's yours," Preston agreed.

WILLOW

"He's not here," Marcus hissed, glaring straight ahead as we sat parked behind an expensive little Mercedes outside his parents' house. It was just as big as I had pictured in my head. The pale-yellow color of the house was set off by large white hurricane shutters. It was beachfront, and the main part of the house started on the second floor. The bottom was all garage. Which made sense, for the Mercedes King of the Gulf Coast to have a large garage. The wide staircase was intimidating, leading up to two large front doors.

Marcus let out an angry growl and opened his door. Something was bothering him, but I was almost afraid to ask. Instead of walking around to get my door, he slammed his door shut and stood glaring up at those large glass-paned doors as if he wanted to rip them off their hinges. As quietly as I could, I opened my door and made my way around the front of his truck. Maybe he was having second thoughts. I knew he was back home due to family issues. But this was much more intense than I'd expected from the perfect family I pictured him to have. Especially after meeting his bubbly, sweet, gorgeous sister. He jerked his head toward me when I stopped beside him, and the angry scowl melted and he frowned.

"I'm sorry, Low. I didn't mean to leave you just sitting in there."

I squeezed his arm. "It's okay. I actually know how to open a car door."

My teasing only brought a hint of a smile to his troubled face.

"My dad was supposed to be here. He's not."

Okay. Missing family meals must really rank high on the shit list around here.

"Mom was expecting him. She was excited." He let out a sigh and reached down to clasp my hand in his.

"If she seems odd or upset, just overlook it. Nothing that happens tonight has anything to do with your presence. Everything is really screwed up right now."

"Trust me, I wrote the book on screwed-up families. I can handle it."

Marcus brought my hand to his mouth and kissed it.

"Let's go see what we're in for tonight," he muttered, and we headed up those massive stairs.

Marcus didn't knock. We walked right in. I guess'd he still

thought of this as his home. Must've been nice. I had to knock at Tawny's. The door was normally locked up tight anyway, and I hadn't been given a key.

"Hello," Marcus called out as he closed the door behind us. Amanda immediately appeared, stepping out of a room up ahead. Her smile faltered and I could tell she was forcing it. I'd done that enough to know it when I saw it.

"Manda," Marcus replied in a cautious tone, "everything good?"

She shrugged, and her gaze flickered to me, then back to him. They needed a moment. I could tell by the pleading in her eyes.

"Could you point me to the restroom?" I asked Marcus, interrupting their silent conversation.

"Yeah, of course." He pointed to a door ahead and to the left. "Just use the powder room."

The powder room? What the crap was a powder room?

"Okay."

Once inside, I sighed and sagged against the wall. Jeez, the tension in this place was thick. I was in the way. Marcus wanting me here was sweet, but now I think he made a mistake. Amanda obviously needed him, and he was saddled with me. And I knew nothing. It bothered me some that he hadn't opened up to me, but then, I hadn't opened up to him either about my family issues. No matter what was going on in this family, it couldn't be worse than what my sister had done. My family issues were not the kind you shared, ever. I needed to kill some time and give them a chance to talk privately.

Looking around the small room, I noticed the sink wasn't a normal sink. It was a fancy cracked glass bowl that sat on top of a marble stand. The faucet looked like a copper spout from a pump. Turning the water on, I was instantly fascinated with the way it worked. Smiling at my childlike fascination with a bathroom sink, I turned the water off and turned my attention to the rest of the room. There was no bathtub or shower. A toilet sat on the other side of me, and a chandelier hung from the tall ceiling. *Who the heck puts a chandelier in a tiny room with nothing but a toilet and a sink?* A knock at the door startled me.

"Low, you okay?" Marcus's voice sounded concerned.

I reached over and opened the door, then grabbed his arm to pull him inside with me. His shocked expression made me want to laugh out loud, but I didn't. The worry lines across his forehead told me he had too much on his mind for fun and games.

"What?" he asked as I closed the door behind him. Turning, I gazed up at his beautiful green eyes. God, he was gorgeous.

"I'm giving you a chance to talk to Amanda alone. She seemed upset," I explained.

He let out a frustrated sigh and nodded.

"I'm sorry about all this," he began, and I put my finger over his mouth to stop him.

"Hush. I know you're having family problems, and your dad not showing up has caused a major hitch in making things better. If my being here makes everyone uncomfortable because they feel as if they have to act happy and as if nothing is wrong, I need to leave. I can call—" Marcus grabbed my finger gently and shook his head.

"No. You aren't calling"—he paused—"anyone. You're staying here with me. I need you here, Low. I'm sorry it's all gone to shit, but I need you here. Please stay with me."

The pleading look in his eyes was my undoing. Of course I would stay with him. I closed the small distance between us and stood up on my tiptoes to kiss him chastely before nodding.

"Then let's go do this."

He grinned for the first time since we'd driven up.

As we walked out of the *powder room*, Amanda was standing there waiting for us with an amused smirk on her face.

"Did ya need to go in there and help her out, Marcus?" she asked with a teasing lilt to her voice.

"Shut up, Manda," he replied, and slipped his arm around my back.

She winked at me before turning around to lead us to the dining room. The table was huge and covered in food. They really did family dinners up right around here. A tall, elegant woman walked out of the kitchen. Her blond hair was almost white. Maybe platinum would be the best way to describe it. It was cut in a short pageboy style that suited her classic appearance. Her slender figure reminded me of Amanda. The white apron tied around her waist was so white it looked as if it had never been used. Underneath the apron she had on what appeared to be a black halter dress complete with black pumps on her feet. When you looked at her, one word came to mind: "rich."

"Marcus." She beamed at the sight of her son.

"Mama, this is Willow." His hand tightened on my waist. "Low, this is my mom, Margaret."

Margaret set the basket of bread down on the table and made her way to me, smiling brightly. A little too brightly. The pain in her eyes was impossible to mask.

"It's so nice to meet you, Willow. I've heard so much about you, and you're just as beautiful as Marcus promised you were."

"It's a pleasure to meet you, too. Thank you so much for inviting me to dinner."

Her smile appeared to relax and become more genuine.

"I'm thrilled you came. Marcus never brings girls to dinner. Your presence is very welcome."

"Can I help you with anything, Mama?"

He called her Mama. How freaking cute was that?

"No, honey, you and Willow have a seat. Amanda is bringing the pitcher of tea, and then we'll be ready."

Marcus pulled out a chair for me, and I sat down while he pushed it back in. Then he walked over and did the same thing for his mother. "Here you go," he said, smiling down at her.

The love in her eyes as she gazed at him was unmistakable. Marcus was very well loved. No matter what his family issues were, his mother and his sister adored him. But then, how could they not?

Chapter Eighteen

MARCUS

My mother prattled on about the upcoming Sea Breeze Seafood Festival and the charity event she was heading up. Willow was perfect. She acted interested in my mother's pointless chatter and even kept the conversation going with questions about the event. Amanda caught my attention twice. She was very happy with Willow. Right now having my mother preoccupied was the best thing, and Willow was doing a fantastic job. It took all my willpower not to lean down and kiss her senseless. When Willow asked if there was anything she could do to help, my mother's face lit up like the Fourth of July. Relief at seeing a real smile on her face made it easier to swallow my food. The sick knot in my stomach at the devastation shining in her eyes when we'd arrived had felt like a lead weight in my stomach. But with each smile Willow brought out of her, I could eat more easily and relax. Amanda's tense posture had also eased. By the end of the meal I'd given up all pretense of not being as fascinated with Willow as my mother was. I openly stared at her, drinking in her smooth skin, the silky hair that curled over her shoulders, and those expressive eyes of hers. The light-pink color in her cheeks told me she knew I was ogling her.

"I'd love to help out. I'll have Marcus text you my number. Then you can let me know when you need me."

She was going to spend time helping my mom. Damn, I was so far gone at this point I'd do anything she asked of me.

"Marcus, honey?" My mother's voice broke into my thoughts and I jerked my gaze off Willow and turned to focus on my mother.

"Yes?"

She chuckled and seemed very pleased. Tonight hadn't been a bust after all. Willow had saved the day.

"Can you help me get the caramel cake and dessert plates, please?"

Nodding, I stood up, and Amanda covered her laughter with a napkin. I had a feeling Mom had called my name more than once before I'd heard her. Both my mother and my sister were way too easily amused. I followed my mother into the kitchen, and the moment we were safely hidden from the dining room, she spun around and hugged me tightly.

"Oh, honey, she's perfect. I love her. She's gorgeous and smart, and you're just so smitten with her. It does my heart so much good to see you like this. And she's local. I'd always worried you'd meet some girl off at college and move away from me. This is perfect. I can't wait to introduce her to the ladies at the club when she comes to help me with the decorations for our booth at the festival."

I couldn't help but laugh at my mother's enthusiasm. My father's no-show was completely forgotten for the moment.

"She's special. I told you that."

"Yes, she's definitely special. I adore her."

"I adore her too, Mama."

Willow had worked the past two nights, and she'd spent all day yesterday at her sister's, keeping Larissa. I was having withdrawals. Tonight I needed her all to myself. We'd have a moonlit picnic on the beach. A little dancing under the stars, and then I was going to make love to her. It was time. I wanted to sleep in a bed with her at night, holding her all night. This couch stuff sucked. But before I dealt with all that, I had to meet with my father. He'd called me twice and left messages, which I'd deleted without listening to. This morning my mother had called me for him. She'd begged me to go see him. She hated having us at odds with each other, which baffled me because he had shattered her world. The woman was just so damn forgiving.

I pulled into his dealership in Sea Breeze. Dad was always at this one. He only visited his other dealerships. This was his home base and largest lot. Taking a deep breath, I stepped out of the truck and headed for the front doors. The curly red hair that belonged to the secretary he supposedly had fired was the first thing I noticed. My scowling at her as I walked past caused her smile to falter, and for the first time in my life I wanted to hurt a woman. I didn't ask if he was in his office. Talking to the whore who had broken up my family wasn't on my to-do list today.

Dad glanced up as I stalked into his office.

"Marcus." He looked surprised.

"Mom asked me to come. I'm here. You got ten minutes."

Frowning, he nodded and motioned for me to sit down. I considered refusing and standing up so I could glare down at him the entire time, but decided it might be safer if I was seated. That way if I lunged for him, he'd have time to duck. Clearing his throat my father loosened his tie and rested both elbows on the desk leaning forward.

"I know my not showing up for the family dinner upset you."

I let out a hard laugh. "No, Dad, the fact that that slut is still working for you when you told Mom you'd fired her is what has me furious at the moment."

His mouth formed a tight line, and I could see my comment about his paid-for toy bothered him.

"Let's leave her out of this, shall we? There are things you don't know, and until you're my age and have walked in my shoes, you'll never understand."

A red haze settled over my vision.

"Your mother and I have been living as roommates for so long, Marcus. She was wrapped up in her world, and I was busy with work, making it possible for her to live the charmed life she's lived. Making it possible for Amanda to have everything she desires. And I'd have done the same for you had you let me. Your refusal to let me help you with anything bothers me. You're my son. I want you to have the best. I can supply the best. But you've fought me every step of the way. That isn't the point." He waved his hand as if swatting those words away. "Your mother and I no longer make each other happy. Our marriage was over long before I moved on. I need affection—"

"Stop," I snarled, standing up. I couldn't listen to this anymore.

"I. Don't. Care. About. Your. Needs." I bit out each word with as much venom in my voice as I could manage. "I only care about the woman who dedicated her life to making a home for Amanda and me. Making a home for you. Nothing she did warranted you running off and fucking a girl half your age. Do you really think she loves you? Really? That's stupid and pathetic. She wants your money, you stupid asswipe."

Dad shot out of his chair, slamming it against the wall behind him. "I will not listen to you call me names. You are my son. I deserve more respect than that."

A sickened, angry laugh bubbled out of me, and I shook my head. "Any respect I may have had for you was killed the moment you betrayed my mother."

I didn't wait for a response. I jerked open his door and slammed it in my wake, needing to let some of my fury loose before I exploded. Customers and salespeople jumped and spun around to stare at the spectacle I was causing. I hoped the customers all left without buying a damn thing. Slicing my heated gaze through the showroom, I found the girl responsible for all this. She was watching me with a shocked, almost fearful expression. I wanted to hurt her. Slam her against a wall and scream at her. But I couldn't. So I settled for words.

"Suck him dry while you can, because you won't be young forever. He'll leave you one day too. For someone younger. A zebra doesn't change his stripes, and I can assure you there is nothing about you that's special. You're just a young piece of ass."

Her jaw dropped open at my words, and I heard gasps from others who'd heard me. Good. My father would think twice before he called and requested I meet with him again.

Storming out of the dealership, I turned my truck toward Live Bay. It was early, but I needed a beer. No, I needed a damn shot of whiskey. Several shots of whiskey.

WILLOW

"Hey, Low." Preston's voice startled me, and I spun around to find him standing behind me with his hands tucked into the pockets of his jeans, frowning.

"Preston, hello."

He glanced around the almost empty restaurant. It was time for me to get off work, and I'd called Marcus but he hadn't answered. I was getting ready to start walking. Calling Cage was out of the question. Maybe Marcus had sent Preston. I sure hoped so. I was exhausted, and walking was the last thing I wanted to do.

"You about done here?" he asked, bringing his attention back to me.

"Yep, I was just about to leave. Did Marcus send you to get me?"

Preston's frown deepened. "Well, not exactly. He's next door at the bar."

He was? Why hadn't he answered my calls? "Okay," I replied, waiting for more of an explanation.

Preston sighed. "He's trashed. Like, drunk off his ass, doesn't know what the hell he's doing, trashed."

Alarmed, I untied my apron, threw it into the dirty basket, and started for the door. Preston followed me.

"Before you see him like this, you should know he met with his dad today and it was brutal. He went directly to the bar and he's been there ever since. He's got a lot of family issues right now, and all the pressure is on him to keep his mom and sister from falling apart. Don't be mad at him. Just understand, okay?"

The pleading tone in Preston's voice scared me. I mentally prepared myself for the worst as I opened the door to the bar and stepped inside, scanning the crowd for my drunk boyfriend.

"Rock has him. I called Rock first. Ginger, the bartender tonight, called me and I called Rock. He came with me."

I found Rock first. He was sitting at a booth off to the side away from the dance floor, and he was alone. I made a bee-line for him. His eyes met mine, and I could see the apologetic expression before he even spoke. My heart was racing in my chest. Where was he? Surely Rock wouldn't let him leave? Drive drunk?

"Where?" I asked the minute I got to his booth.

Rock pointed his mug toward the dance floor. Spinning around, I immediately found him.

He was dancing with Jess, and she was humping his leg while he held on to her hips and grinned like he was having the time of his life. Furious, I stalked out onto the dance floor. That bitch had pushed me too far. I didn't care whose cousin she was. I'd had it. Marcus was mine. His bloodshot green eyes met mine as I stopped behind Jess. Grabbing her shoulder, I jerked her back with all the strength I could muster. I heard her shocked squeal as she stumbled back.

"Baby," Marcus slurred, reaching for me. "My Low's here." His garbled words were muffled as he pulled me against him, burying his head in my neck.

Fingernails bit into my arm. I cried out in pain, startling Marcus, whose head jerked up, looking confused and unstable.

"Back off, bitch," Jess shrilled behind me. Pushing Marcus

back just enough so he didn't end up getting in the way of any blows that were about to happen, I turned around and glared at her.

"I suggest you back off. Touching my boyfriend like that is not cool with me. He's drunk. He won't remember this tomorrow. So back the hell off before I break that perfect little nose job of yours," I hissed, taking another step toward her.

She cackled. "I'm not scared of you."

I raised one eyebrow and smirked. "Really? Well, princess, you ever got into a fight with a girl from my side of town? We don't fight fair. I won't pull your hair and scratch your face. We fight to live. You'll wake up flat on your back on this dance floor. Want to see if I'm bluffing? Please, by all means, take a swing at me. You start it, and I'll finish it."

I heard chanting and a few catcalls and whistles, but I ignored everything. Blocking out the crowd was the first rule. I could take her down. I had no doubt. Cage had taught me to street fight at a young age. The indecision in her face as I held her gaze, unflinching and waiting, was laughable.

"Back off, Jess." Rock came up behind her, taking both her arms and pulling her back. She didn't fight him. She went willingly, turning around and letting him lead her out the front door. Once they were outside, I turned around to see Marcus's glassy stare focused on me, a goofy grin on his face. Yep, he was completely wasted.

"That was hot, Low," he slurred, reaching out and pulling me against him.

He smelled like Cage. I didn't like it. I wanted my Marcus back. Pushing against his chest, I stared up at him. A frown puckered his brow.

"What's wrong?" he asked, swaying slightly.

Telling him what was wrong was pointless.

"I'm taking you home," I replied, and grabbed his arm, slipping mine through his to help keep him straight.

Preston met us at the door and opened it.

"I'm sorry you had to see him like this," Preston whispered.

I nodded. I was sorry I'd had to see it too. I was also sorry I'd had to go all badass in a bar full of people. I remembered Preston's reasons why Marcus was drunk, but I had a hard time accepting it. So what! He'd had an argument with his dad. Well, he had a mother and sister who loved him. I didn't even have that, but you didn't see me running off to get drunk every time my sister and I fought. Which was every time I saw her. No, he didn't have an excuse for this. Nor did he have an excuse for letting another girl hump his leg. And his hands had been on her waist. His big hands had been mere inches from her massive tits. For all I knew, he could have copped a feel before I'd arrived tonight.

"He just has some family problems," Preston said as he opened the passenger door of Marcus's truck. I let him help

Marcus in and buckle him up, and then I closed the door.

"I'm the poster child for family problems. But do you know how many times I've been drunk? None. Not one time. I realize he's your friend and you're protecting him, but the fact remains that he got drunk and had his hands all over another girl. She was humping him rather hard, I might add. Do you think he'd have been okay with things if the situation was reversed? No! I can tell you he'd have lost it. I'm going to take him home. I'll put him to bed and deal with it in the morning. But please, Preston, no more excuses. He doesn't have one that will fly in my book."

Preston let out a long sigh and nodded, stepping back so I could walk around to the driver's side of the truck.

"Oh, here's his keys. I took them off him when I got here." Preston threw me the keys. "He really does love you," he said, then held up his hands in surrender. "Don't yell at me. That's all I'm saying. I'll shut up now."

I managed to give him a tight smile that I did not feel before getting into the truck and driving us home.

Chapter Nineteen

MARCUS

I couldn't swallow. There was cotton in my throat and a pretty thick coating of it on my tongue, too. Smacking my mouth, I started to move, and my head screeched in rebellion. Falling back onto the soft bed underneath me, I moaned. What was wrong with me? Slowly I peeled my eyelids up, and the sun peeked through the blinds on my window. Confused, I glanced down at myself. I was wearing jeans and a T-shirt. I was in my bed. Something was wrong. Pressing my head between my palms, I forced myself to sit up. The room started spinning and I closed my eyes. I knew this feeling. It had been a while since I'd had it, but I knew what it was. Massive hangover. Noise on the other side of the door helped me focus. I was in my room. Why was I in my room? How had I gotten to my room?

Willow. Standing up, I forced my feet to move until I opened the door to my room. Then I leaned against it and groaned at the dizzy spell caused by the pain in my head.

"You look like shit."

Opening my eyes, I found Cage walking into the living room with a cup of coffee in his hands. Swinging my attention to the couch, I noticed it was empty. Willow. Where was Willow?

"You're also a really bad drunk."

Shit. What had I done?

"Low," I managed to say through the worst case of dry mouth I'd ever had.

Cage sat down on the couch and smirked at me. What was so damn funny?

"Low's in my bed."

What? Why? She wouldn't do that. She knows I don't want her in there. Pushing off from the door, I started for Cage's bedroom.

"Leave her alone. She needs sleep. Last night wasn't exactly easy on her."

I stopped and turned to look back at him.

"What happened?"

Cage raised his eyebrows at me and the smirk on his face had vanished and he looked pissed.

"You want a complete recap? Okay." Cage leaned forward, resting his elbows on his knees, and glared at me.

"Low came to get your drunk ass from the bar last night. When she got there, you were all but screwing Jess on the dance floor. Hands all over her. Low went and snatched Jess off you, and then when Jess proceeded to threaten her, Low basically called her bullshit and sent her packing. From what I hear, it was damn hot. Anyway, she then hauled your drunk ass home. You passed out in your truck. She had to get me to help her get you up the stairs and into bed. Then she proceeded to break down on me and cry. I cuddled her up in my arms like I always do when she's hurting and carried her to my bed, where she told me all of this and then promptly fell asleep. Preston called and gave me the whole story as well."

I was going to be sick. What had I done? My chest ached, my stomach rolled, and my head pounded. I'd sent her running into Cage's arms for comfort—again. I'd been the reason Jess had threatened her. I'd put her in danger and she'd taken care of me.

DAMMIT!

Dropping into the chair nearest to me, I cradled my spinning head in my hands and fought the urge to cry like a damn baby.

"I thought I'd kill you when you hurt her, you know. But damned if I'm not just relieved that it's over. I don't even want to hurt you. I'm just so happy to have her back."

That was all it took. I ran for the toilet and lost everything in my stomach. Several times. Then I slid down the wall and cried silently. It all came back to my father. He was the reason I had gotten drunk. If I lost Willow over this, I'd kill him. I couldn't lose her. The idea hurt so bad it made breathing impossible.

The bathroom door opened slowly, and I turned to look up at a very solemn Willow. I soaked in the sight of her as she stepped inside and closed the door behind her. She handed me a cold washcloth. "Here."

I took it, unable to take my eyes off her as I washed the cold sweat from my face. Then she handed me the glass in her hands.

"Drink this. It'll help."

Taking it, I took several small sips and watched her, afraid she'd turn and leave. But she didn't. Instead, she slid down the wall and sat beside me.

"I'm sorry. I'm so, so damn sorry," I choked out.

She didn't respond. Instead, she sat there staring down at her hands clasped tightly in her lap. I wanted to pull her in my arms and hold her. Keep her from leaving me. But I could smell the whiskey and smoke on my clothes. I stunk.

"You hurt me," she finally replied in a small voice. What little part of my heart was still in one piece shattered at her words. The lump in my throat constricted my airways.

"God, Low, I'm so sorry." I wanted to profess my love but right now that sounded unbelievable. I didn't want those words to be tainted by this.

"I understand that you had a fight with your father. Preston explained that. But, Marcus, what I don't understand is why you'd go drink so much that you were dancing and touching another woman. My sister and I fight all the time. I don't have a mom and sister like you do who love me. I have no family. The only family I have hates me. Larissa doesn't count because she's a baby. I know family problems suck, Marcus. I have major problems. Things you don't know about. Issues that are eating me up inside. But none of that is an excuse for me to run off and get trashed and rub all over another guy."

I was a selfish, spoiled brat. She was right. If the roles had been reversed, I'd have been a madman. I wouldn't be sitting beside her talking calmly the next morning. She was too good for me. I'd already figured this out, but now I knew how undeserving I was.

"You're right. I don't deserve you."

Willow's hand reached out and covered mine, and my body trembled from her touch. Shit, I was going to cry right in front of her. Fighting the burn of tears in my eyes, I couldn't look at her. Slowly I moved my thumb and hooked it through hers. I wasn't brave enough to completely take her hand. I couldn't handle it if she jerked it away.

"Don't ever do that to me again."

Her words sank in slowly, and I turned my head to meet her gaze, no longer caring that my eyes were watery from unshed tears.

"Again? You mean you forgive me? It's not over?" I asked in disbelief.

She smiled and turned her hand over, and threaded her fingers through mine, holding them tightly.

"I forgive you," she said, then reached out with her other hand and wiped the moisture in my eyelashes away. "How do I stay mad at this? Hmm? You sitting here on the bathroom floor fighting back tears and looking completely defeated." She shifted closer and laid her head on my shoulder. "I love you, Marcus. Of course I forgive you." Setting the glass in my hand down on the edge of the tub, I reached for her and pulled her into my arms. I needed to hold her. I'd almost lost her and I needed her close. She curled up against me, and tears of relief rolled freely down my face.

"I love you, too. So much, Low. So very much. I promise you, Low, I'll never hurt you again."

WILLOW

Over the next week Marcus went out of his way to do sweet, romantic things for me. I came home from work one night to a candlelit bubble bath waiting on me. He left sweet little notes all over the place for me. A customer had even delivered one to me during work one night. I'd awakened twice to find a vintage Aerosmith concert T-shirt beside my pillow. One was a 1984 California, and the other a 1986 Aero-Force One.

I was ready to take the next step, but I was waiting on him. He needed to reassure himself that I wasn't leaving him. That he'd won my forgiveness. He had, of course. We'd led two very different lives. It wasn't fair of me to expect him to handle bad situations the same way I did. He'd grown up protected from bad situations. He didn't know how to roll with the punches. I'd been so eaten up with jealousy I'd wanted to punish him. I didn't want there to have been a reason for him to behave the way he had. You can't expect a sheltered person to react to disappointment the way someone who'd only known disappointment reacted.

Stepping outside into the sunshine after being shut up in a classroom all day, I lifted my face to the sunshine and inhaled the salty breeze. Summer would be here soon, and I couldn't wait to spend it with Marcus. Cage was planning a two-week road trip with some of his friends. He wanted me to come too, but I was looking forward to those two weeks alone with Marcus. This would be the first time Cage and I would be apart for that long. It worried me some, but the fear of being left alone was beginning to wane. Since the morning I'd seen the tears in Marcus's eyes when he thought he'd lost me, I'd felt more secure in our relationship. He loved me just as fiercely as I loved him. I no longer doubted that. Calling Cage when I needed someone never even crossed my mind anymore. The first person I wanted was Marcus. Besides, Marcus bought my Jarritos now. He never let them get low enough for Cage to notice. He kept me so well stocked it was comical. Cage had grumbled about it at first, but he'd gotten over it.

My happy thoughts were interrupted when my eyes landed on my sister standing against a new Mercedes SUV smiling like the cat who caught the canary. Or more like the cat who caught the rich old dude. Walking toward her, I frowned, taking in her new wheels. I wondered if it had been purchased from one of Marcus's dad's lots.

"Tawny," I said, stopping in front of her.

"Like the car?" Tawny all but purred from pleasure. No. I didn't like the way she'd gotten it. But I did like the fact that Larissa would no longer be hauled around in that death trap of my sister's.

"You got it by spreading your legs, sis. I'm not a fan of home wreckers."

She rolled her eyes and gave me a disgusted look. As if I was the gross one. Hello, Miss Screwing-Someone-Twice-Your-Age.

"Whatever. I wanted to let you know I'm moving and I'm selling the house. Jefferson feels like it's best. Letting you have it is pointless. You don't live there. It's mine anyway. Mom left it to me."

This information stung, but I'd expected it. She'd never given me anything. Why start now?

"Where are you moving to?" It had better not be far.

I couldn't care less about Tawny, but Larissa was my niece. I wanted to be able to see her.

Tawny smirked and tilted her head so that her copper curls draped over her bare arm. "Jefferson is moving us to Mobile. He has a nice big house bought for us, and he is moving in with us as soon as the ink is dry on his divorce papers."

An hour away. Not bad, but still farther than I liked. At least Tawny would have no need to work. She would be home with Larissa, and maybe this lifestyle would ignite the mother in her. Maybe she and Larissa could bond. I swallowed the bitter taste in my mouth. Tawny was really breaking up a marriage. But Larissa would have a daddy. I was so torn. Knowing Larissa wouldn't have to live the life I'd had was such a relief. But knowing a marriage had been destroyed, another family was losing their father, broke my heart. God, could this be any more screwed up?

"Here." Tawny handed me an envelope. I reached out to take it. It had my name written on the outside in Tawny's swirly handwriting, and it was sealed.

"It's some money. For all the times you kept Larissa and so you can get a place of your own and move out of Cage York's bed. I also put our new address in there. Larissa will want to see you." I stared at my sister, dumbfounded. Who was this and what had she done with Tawny?

"You're giving me money?" I asked incredulously.

She straightened her shoulders, and I could see the mask of indifference take its place on her face. Tawny didn't do emotion.

"I always pay my debts, Low." She flashed me her beauty-queen smile and flipped her hair over her shoulders. "Well, I have to go meet my fiancé and pick Larissa up from the sitter." She turned to saunter off, then stopped and glanced back over her shoulder. "You're smart, Low. Do something with that."

I just stood there as she climbed into her fancy new SUV and drove off. What had just happened? Had that been her way of saying she was sorry? Looking down at the envelope in my hands, I opened it carefully. Pulling out a check for ten thousand dollars, I stared at it in shock. Then my eyes focused on who the check was from:

Jefferson M. Hardy II
Mercedes Benz of the Gulf Coast

Chapter Twenty

MARCUS

I couldn't find Willow anywhere. She wasn't answering her phone or responding to my texts. Her class was over hours ago. I searched through her things, looking for her sister's phone number. Nothing.

My phone dinged, and I scrambled to grab it. A text from Amanda. Not what I'd been hoping for.

"Mom needs you. Hurry, please."

Shit.

I needed to find Willow. I didn't have time for family drama. Dad no doubt had done something new and sent Mom into a spiraling mess.

"Where are you, Low?" I growled in frustration, staring

down at my phone and trying to decide who to call. Who would know where she was?

"I'm here." Her voice was so soft I almost didn't hear her over the chaos in my head. I spun around and found her standing in our bedroom doorway. She looked devastated.

"What's wrong?" I asked, rushing to her and pulling her into my arms. Swollen red eyes and a tear-streaked face were just the beginning of what was wrong with her. Her arms didn't embrace me in return. Instead, she stood limp.

"Low, you're scaring me," I said into her hair, needing some kind of reaction from her.

She didn't respond.

My phone went off again and I ignored it. Tightening my hold on her, I waited, hoping she'd say something. Anything.

My phone started ringing. Frustrated, I grabbed it and started to decline it when I saw it was Amanda. Something had to really be wrong.

"What, Manda? I'm busy at the moment."

"She's taken something, Marcus! Help me!" Her screams came through the phone so loud Willow jerked in my arms. She'd heard her.

"Who? Mom took something?" My heart was pounding in my chest. Oh, God, no.

"YES! She won't wake up. I called 911 but I can't find a pulse! Help me!" she wailed.

"I'm coming. Keep her alive, Manda. You hear me!? Keep her breathing. Do mouth-to-mouth. Something!"

Willow had stood back from my embrace, and her face was chalk white. I needed to deal with what was bothering her, but my mother's life hung in the balance right now and I couldn't.

"Low, I gotta go."

She nodded. "Hurry," she said frantically. I could see the horror in her eyes. She'd heard every word Amanda had said. She understood. I wasn't leaving her. She knew that. I bolted for the door. Please, God, don't let my mama die.

Five hours later my mother's stomach had been pumped and she was being given fluids through an IV. My sister hadn't been able to find a pulse because in her panic she wasn't looking in the right place. But she had been right about one thing. Mom had taken a bottle of pain pills. The divorce papers had been signed by my dad, and were clutched against her chest when I'd gotten there.

Mom's eyes flickered open, and she focused on me. I moved from my stance against the wall where I'd stood for over an hour watching her, willing her to open her eyes. "Marcus," she whispered. I grabbed her hand and nodded. Suddenly I wasn't a twenty-one-year-old man. I was a little boy. Scared and in need of his mama to hold him and tell him everything was going to be okay. Seeing them lift her lifeless body onto the gurney and take her from the house was a nightmare I never wanted to relive.

"I'm sorry," she whispered.

"Shh, Mama. Don't talk. It's okay. Just promise you'll never do that to me again. I can't handle that, Mama. I can't." I squeezed her hand and she let out a small sob. I didn't want her to cry. Not now. She needed to recover.

"He left me. Took her with him. Moved to Mobile," she said in a hoarse whisper.

I reached for the glass of water and straw the nurse had left a few minutes ago. She'd said Mom would need it when she woke up.

"Here, Mama, take a small sip. I don't want to talk about him. He's gone. We're all still here, and we aren't going anywhere."

She obediently took a small sip of water and laid her head back against the pillow.

"I love you," she said, staring up at me with sad eyes.

"I love you, too. Manda and I need you, Mama. You can't try to leave us again. We need you." I spoke gently but forcefully. I needed her to understand that even though our father had cast her off, we never would. She was important to us.

"I need you, too."

I nodded. "Good. Now take another drink."

227

"You're awake."

I glanced back as Amanda ran toward the bed and hovered over our broken mother. "Oh, Mama, you're okay. You're awake," she gushed.

Mom reached for Amanda's hand and grasped it.

"I'm sorry. I won't do this ever again. I had a weak moment," she explained slowly, looking up at my sister. Amanda sniffed back tears before crawling up on the bed and curling up beside Mom.

"My baby girl," Mom cooed, and kissed Amanda's forehead.

They were here and they were safe. It was going to be okay. I could do this. I could hold this family together. I'd do whatever I had to do. Low would help me. Mom loved her. We'd make it through this.

WILLOW

Cage saw me the minute he exited the dugout. Frowning, he made his way over to me. I'd never come to one of his practices before. I could see the question and concern on his face.

"Low, what's wrong?" he asked when he reached me. I felt the sob inside me well up, and I covered my mouth to silence it. His eyes widened and he reached for my hand.

"Come on," he said, pulling me with him, away from the curious eyes of his teammates. He led us straight to his car and opened the passenger side door. "Get in."

I didn't argue. I climbed in. The familiar smell of safety surrounded me, and my eyes filled with tears. Cage would always be my safe place. Because once Marcus knew the truth, I was going to lose him. He was going to leave me too. And I didn't blame him.

Cage climbed into the driver's seat, then turned to look at me.

"What happened, and whose ass do I need to beat?"

I shook my head. "No one's. Oh, Cage, it's awful. It's worse than I could've ever even imagined."

"Nothing's that bad, baby. Ever. And if it is, I'll fix it."

"You can't fix this, Cage. This is unfixable."

"Nothing's unfixable."

"Larissa and Marcus have the same father!" I yelled, fisting my hands over my eyes as another sob rattled my chest.

Silence.

I'd rendered him speechless.

"The married man Tawny's been screwing is Marcus's father. Jefferson *HARDY* just left his wife for my sister."

"Fuck."

I dropped my hands into my lap and looked at Cage's horrified expression.

"How do you know? I mean, how did you find out? Does Marcus know?"

"She met me outside my class today. Driving a brand-new Mercedes SUV. Told me that Larissa's daddy had left his wife and they were moving to Mobile. He'd bought them a fancy new house and he was moving in with them. Then she handed me a check for what she called the debt she owed me and left." I reached into my pocket, pulled out the check, and handed it to Cage.

"Holy Mother."

"Look who wrote me the check, Cage. Not the amount."

He lifted his blue eyes to me. "Low, baby, I'm so sorry. She just keeps fucking your life up."

"I knew he had family problems, and I knew he hated his dad and he was worried about his mother. But God, Cage, I'd never in a million years have guessed this."

Cage reached over and grasped my hand in his. "I'm here. You got me. You know that."

I knew that. But it wasn't my losing Cage I was worried about.

"I need to talk to her, him, both of them. I need to go see Tawny and Jefferson, Marcus's dad. I have to find a way to tell Marcus and not lose him. I can't lose him, Cage."

Cage cranked up the car. "Buckle up and type their address into my GPS." I quickly did as I was told, then laid my head back on the seat, closed my eyes, and prayed I'd find a way to make this okay.

It was dark when we pulled up to the large two-story brick home inside the gated golf course community where my sister and niece now lived. Cage pulled into their driveway, and I sat staring up at the home in front of me. Lights were on in almost every room of the house. They were here. It was time to find some answers. To understand what had happened. I just needed some way to keep Marcus. I glanced down at my phone again. Marcus hadn't texted me since his last text two hours ago telling me his mother was doing fine. He hadn't explained what had happened. I thought I'd heard his sister say something about calling 911, but apparently that hadn't happened. Amanda must've overreacted. If his mother had gone to the hospital, he'd have told me. He'd have wanted me there.

"Come on. Let's go do this," Cage said, opening my car door. I'd been so lost in thought I hadn't even noticed he'd gotten out of the car. I stood up, and we walked to the front double doors together. Seeing those two large double doors reminded me of the other house this man owned. The one where he'd raised Amanda and Marcus. The one he'd abandoned.

I reached out and pressed the doorbell, then waited.

Jefferson Hardy opened the door. Surprise lit his eyes as he stood back.

"Willow, please come in. Larissa was just talking about you."

He remembered my name.

I stepped inside and Cage was right behind me.

"Who is it?" Tawny asked as she appeared at the top of the large elegant wooden staircase. She froze and her gaze shifted from me to Cage and back.

"Low, what're you doing here?"

She was annoyed. Good. I was devastated.

"I need to talk to you." I turned to look back at Jefferson. "And him."

Jefferson and Tawny exchanged looks while I waited.

"Okay, well, Tawny, why don't you get Larissa and come on down here. She'll be thrilled to see Willow." This man was playing house so easily. As if he hadn't just abandoned another family. The one he'd had for more years than Tawny had been alive.

"Follow me," Jefferson said, smiling at me, and then turned to lead us down a hallway and into a large living room already furnished with several large leather chairs big enough for two and a huge sectional sofa. The largest flat-screen I'd ever seen hung on the wall, and a gas fire crackled in the fireplace. Wasn't this just cozy?

"Can I offer you something to drink?" Jefferson asked.

I shook my head.

"No" was Cage's only reply. I felt like he was my bodyguard. It helped knowing he was here.

"My Lowlow," Larissa squealed in obvious delight when Tawny walked into the room carrying Larissa on her hip. Her hair was damp from a bath and she was in a pair of pajamas I'd never seen before. They looked soft, frilly, and expensive. Seeing Larissa in something so nice just added to the mass of emotions swirling around inside me. I wanted the best for Larissa. I wanted her to have a daddy who loved her and was there for her. But what about the other little girl this man had? The teenage one who was falling apart from his betrayal. I wanted to scream in frustration.

Tawny put Larissa down, and she ran to me, her arms up in the air. I bent down and picked her up and nuzzled her sweet neck. She smelled so good. Like a baby should smell. A healthy, loved baby.

"Hey, my favorite princess," I whispered in her ear.

"Lowlow." She smiled up at me.

"I missed you," I told her, and she clapped happily and then planted a wet kiss on my cheek.

"*Cay!*" she squealed when her eyes found Cage, and she wiggled in my arms to get to him.

"Hey, gorgeous," he replied, taking her from my arms.

I turned to look back at my sister and Jefferson.

"I didn't know until today who you were, exactly," I said, staring straight at Jefferson.

"It wasn't your business, Low," Tawny snapped, coming to stand beside him, wrapping her arm around his.

"That's where you're wrong. It unfortunately is my business."

"Larissa is mine and Jefferson's. Just because we—"

"Tawny, shut up. You have no idea what I came here to say. So just let me talk. For once." I watched as my sister's eyes glowed with anger. Jefferson patted her hand soothingly.

"Let's hear her out, sweetheart."

I closed my eyes, wishing with everything I had that I could reverse this. That I could stop this. That Larissa could belong to another man. An unmarried man who would love her and take care of her. Not this one.

"Cage, can you and Larissa go exploring, please?" I asked, not looking back at him.

"Yep."

I saw Jefferson's displeasure.

"He's taken care of your daughter more times than you have. I can assure you, she's in very good hands." I hadn't won a fan with that comment, but it was a fact. "Today when I got that check, I saw Jefferson's last name for the first time. You had never mentioned it to me before. And you always refused to tell me where you worked. I figured it was because the affair you were having was with someone at work."

"I didn't tell you because it wasn't your business," Tawny snarled.

"Again, that's where you're wrong. You see, something has happened that makes this a very real issue for me. I hated knowing you were tearing a family apart. I hated knowing you were destroying another marriage."

"My marriage has been over a long time, Willow," Jefferson began.

I glared up at him. "Really? Because when you didn't show up to the family dinner your wife had so lovingly prepared and your daughter and son had shown up for expecting to see their father, it destroyed them. I watched it. I witnessed your wife put on a smile that didn't match the heartbreak in her eyes. I watched your son's hatred for you grow even stronger and I watched your daughter—the other one, who still needs her daddy, especially right now—while her world is falling apart, do everything she could to make her mother and brother smile. I had a front-row seat, Mr. Hardy."

"What in the hell are you ranting about, Low?" Tawny yelled over me.

"I met a guy. For the first time in my life I fell in love. I let down my walls. I found someone who makes me laugh. Who gives me hope. I love him with everything I have in me. But he's dealing with a mother who's completely shattered. A little sister who is scared. He's doing all he can to fix it for them. While his father is off playing house with *you*."

"Marcus," Jefferson said with a heavy sigh. He understood. He got it.

"Yes, Marcus," I replied, still glaring at my sister. "So you see the predicament I'm in. I love Marcus Hardy so much that I'd give up anything for him. *Anything*. Anything but Larissa. I can't see a way out of this. He won't have anything to do with me when he finds this out. My sister is the reason his family is destroyed. The reason he got a call today from his frantic sister because something was wrong with his mother."

I let out a hard laugh and then screamed, throwing my hands up in the air.

"You're in love with Jeff's son?"

I swung around and my eyes shot daggers at Tawny.

"Yes."

"Just leave, Low. Your dramatic performance has ruined my evening. I'm sorry you're so worked up about this, but it isn't our problem."

"Tawny, don't be so callous," Jefferson said, looking down at her.

"Callous? Jeff, this is utterly ridiculous. She thinks she loves your son, and if she thinks coming over here and ranting about us is going to make a difference, she's sadly mistaken."

A chime went through the house, and I paused.

"Who else is here? My God, we just moved in."

Tawny stormed off to answer the door, and I stood staring blankly into the fire. She was right. What good was this doing? I wasn't going to get an answer by sharing with them how royally they'd screwed up so many lives. They simply didn't care. And even if they did, what did I expect them to do about it?

"Low." Marcus's voice broke into my thoughts, and I jerked my gaze from the fire to find Tawny standing in the living room entrance with her arms crossed over her chest and scowling.

"Look who else is here," Tawny spat, walking back to Jefferson and staking her claim by slipping her arm around his.

"Marcus." I didn't know what else to say. I just stood there and watched the whole awful scene unfold. His eyes shifted from Tawny to me. I knew the moment he saw it. The resemblance. It was unmistakable. Especially with us standing in the same room. The emotions on his face went from shock to pain to despair to fury within seconds.

"You're her sister. This is—" He stopped and looked at his dad. "Oh, God, no." He started shaking his head. "Larissa. She's not. She can't be."

He was shattered. I could see the moment it happened. I knew the feeling. I'd just experienced it myself.

"Martus pay," Larissa squealed when Cage walked into the room holding her.

Marcus looked back at Larissa with horror in his eyes. Then he looked at me, and I could see the betrayal there. He thought I'd known all along. I could see it as he just stared at me. Larissa continued to try to get his attention by chanting his name and demanding he play.

Marcus stared at me as his anger turned to numbness. The tic in his jaw and his rigid stance only grew more severe the longer we stood there staring at each other. I could feel him slipping away with each second, but there was nothing I could say. I didn't know how to stop this. How to explain.

"You. Are. Dead. To. Me," he said in a hard, emotionless voice. Then he turned and left. Those short, clipped words woke me up from my trance. I ran after him.

"Marcus, wait! Please wait!" I called out, but he didn't stop. He didn't look back.

"MARCUS, PLEASE!" I screamed as he opened the front door. This time he paused and slowly turned around. The hatred in his eyes directed at me was crippling.

"Do you know where I've been, Willow? Of course you don't. You've been here with your sister and my father playing house. While I've been by my mother's hospital bed. As she recovered from an overdose of painkillers that she took after receiving the divorce papers my father so thoughtfully brought to the house today to inform her he was leaving her for another woman. That's where I've been all day. So please don't say one more word. I never want to see you or even hear your name again. I'll be completely moved out of the apartment in a matter of hours. Stay away until I'm gone. If you ever felt anything for me at all. Stay. Away. From. Me."

Chapter Twenty-One

MARCUS

Two Months Later

"A sober Marcus Hardy? I do believe my eyes deceive me," Dewayne drawled as I pulled out a chair and sat down beside Rock at the table they'd taken over at Live Bay to hear Jackdown perform.

"He just got here. It's early yet. Give him time," Preston chimed in as he plopped back down with a girl apparently attached to him. She wiggled on his lap and he licked her ear. Usual Preston behavior. The tourists were piling in, and there was fresh meat everywhere. Preston would screw his way through the best-looking ones for the next three months.

"I'm not drinking tonight. I dropped out of all my classes this semester before I failed them. So I figure it's time I sober up and play makeup with a few summer courses."

Rock patted me on the back. "There's the old Marcus we know and love. Knew you were in there somewhere. Glad you're back."

I didn't look over at him. Because I wasn't back. I was just as dead inside sober as I was drunk. The old Marcus had been completely destroyed. Never to return.

"Smile, brother, there are hot, barely clothed girls crawling all over this place. And all they want are one-night stands. It's freaking heaven on earth," Preston said, grinning like a little boy in a candy store.

"Screwing faceless girls is getting old. I need a break from them, too," I said, and turned down the beer a waitress offered me. I had a bottled water. It was going to take a lot of water to cleanse me of all the alcohol I'd forced on myself.

"Break from pussy? Whatever, man," Dewayne replied with disbelief.

"I thought you were going on that road trip with, uh—" Rock asked Preston.

"You can say his name. I'm not an idiot, and I don't care. How many times do I have to tell you that it doesn't matter to me?" I snapped.

"Okay, um, so that road trip you were talking about with Cage. You decided to pass it up?"

Preston shrugged. "I don't know. Cage seems to be backing out of it. He's kind of changed lately." He trailed off, and

I could feel the tension at the table. They were so worried that one mention of Willow would send me into a blind rage. I was past that. Sure, I'd gone a little mental at the mention of her name or anything that reminded me of her for a while, but I was over it. Completely numb where she was concerned.

I leaned back in my chair and watched as the sea of people danced. No one caught my attention. No one stood out to me. I was numb to more than just Willow. I was numb to life. She'd completely messed me up. But I'd survived. I was better now. I wasn't a brainless sap anymore, and no female would ever have that much control over me again.

"Uh, Marcus, man, you sure you're all good with Willow and stuff now?" Dewayne asked.

I glared at him. Why'd he have to keep saying her name and bringing it up?

"Yes."

He nodded. "Good, 'cause she just walked in lookin' like a damn goddess."

I hadn't seen her since the night I'd left her standing in my father's new home. I'd avoided her at all costs, and she'd done the same. Not once had she stepped foot into the bar. I tried not to look for her. I told myself I didn't give a shit. But I was weak and I turned my head toward the door.

She'd lost weight.

Her hair was longer.

She had on a new dress that clung to every curve.

She was breathtaking.

And she was wrapped up in Cage York's arms.

I'd heard he didn't go out much anymore. I knew it was because of Willow. I'd told myself he was just being her friend. That he was still sleeping around, just not as much. But the possessive gleam in his eyes as he kept her pulled up against his side told me something else. I wanted to look away. And damn, I wanted not to care. She was a liar. Cut from the same cloth as her whore sister. That's what I'd tried to convince myself over the past weeks. It never sounded believable. Even though I'd caught her there. There were so many things about her that screamed she was nothing like her sister. Watching her as she looked nervously up at Cage as he spoke to her. He was her safety net. Just like he'd predicted. I'd left her and she'd had Cage to run back to. But she hadn't stood by and lied to Cage either. She hadn't watched as her sister tore his family apart. *No*. She'd done all that to me. She'd claimed to love me, then let her sister almost destroy my mother. My sister. Me.

Cage bent down and whispered in her ear, and a small smile lifted the corners of her mouth. Then her head turned and her eyes locked with mine. The smile vanished and she froze. Her hand flew up to grab Cage's arm as if she needed his protection, and rage ignited in me. She wasn't going to destroy me again. It was my turn. I stood up and grabbed the tipsy brunette in Preston's lap.

"Come on, baby, dance with me." I didn't wait to see Low's reaction. My dance partner scrambled out of Preston's lap and clung to me, obviously happy with this turn of events. Closing off my feelings and shutting down my emotions, I pulled her against me and moved against her. I cupped her barely covered ass, and she purred and pressed closer to me. I'd show Willow. She wanted to show up here with Cage? Well, baby, you can look your eyes full. The girl's arms ran up my chest and clasped around my neck. I smiled down at her, focusing on her face and trying my damnedest to get Willow's image out of my head.

"All right, man, you accomplished what you set out to do," Preston said, pulling the brunette off me. "She turned and fled. Congrats. Now give me back my date." I didn't even try to hold on to her. I looked back at the door. Willow was gone.

WILLOW

Cage walked into the living room holding a large bowl of popcorn and two sodas. I'd stopped drinking Jarritos. They reminded me of Marcus too much. I pulled back the blanket to let Cage under it with me. Once we had it covering us up, he put the bowl in his lap and handed me a soda.

"I'm agreeing to this chick flick shit because tonight sucked. But the next movie is going to have some blood and action. Got it?"

I laughed and nodded. Cage was beyond wonderful.

"Pinkie promise," I said, holding out my pinkie. Cage looked down at it and then back at me with a mischievous grin before pulling it into his mouth and sucking it.

"Cage!" I squealed, pulling it out of his mouth with a pop.

"Don't point your cute little body parts at me and I won't suck on them," he replied with a wink.

I never would have made it through the past two months without Cage. My chest still ached and my anxiety attacks were back full force, but I was actually doing better. Well, until Cage had talked me into facing everyone at Live Bay tonight. I'd thought I was ready. But Marcus had been there. He'd looked at me and I'd thought for a moment I saw relief as our gazes locked. But I'd been way off base. He'd jumped up and taken a girl onto the dance floor and begun to grope her right there for my viewing pleasure. He'd been sending me a message, and I'd gotten it loud and clear. Cage had spun me around and hauled me out of there so quick I didn't have time to fall apart.

"Eat. I've loaded this down with butter and salt. You're doing better. Putting on a little more weight. I don't want you to relapse after tonight."

I reached into the bowl, grabbed a large handful of popcorn, and stuffed it into my mouth.

Cage chuckled. "Awesome."

Chewing, I settled in against Cage's side and focused on the movie. If I didn't concentrate, I'd think about all the times I'd spent with Marcus on this couch. How many times I'd watched him sleep right here where we sat. It seemed like forever ago now. Almost like that part of my life was a dream. Tonight reminded me that it wasn't. It was very real. And just like before, the person I'd loved had left me. I reached over and grasped Cage's shirt tightly in my hand. I needed the reminder that I loved Cage and he hadn't left. Not when I'd lost it and completely shattered after Marcus had left me standing there at my sister's. Not when the panic attacks started happening every night. He'd stayed. Given up his nights out so he could take care of me. He was my family. He was all I had. Facing my sister was impossible. I missed Larissa so much it hurt, but I couldn't go back there. The memories attached to that house were too painful. One day I'd be okay. Then I'd go see my niece. I'd learn to accept what my sister had done and accept Jefferson Hardy as Larissa's father.

"He still cares."

Cage's words startled me.

"What?" I asked, looking back to the screen, thinking he was commenting on what was happening.

"Marcus. He cares, Low. I saw it in his eyes. What he did tonight was shitty, but it was his defense mechanism. He doesn't want to care. But he does."

I shook my head and closed my eyes. I didn't want to hear that. Not now.

"No, Cage. Don't. I can't let myself hope. He hates me. He always will."

Cage clicked his tongue. "There's a thin line, baby. A thin line between love and hate."

"No. There isn't."

Cage tucked the hair that had come loose from my braid behind my ear.

"Low, a guy doesn't fall in love with you and have you love him back, then just throw it away. You're too special. After being loved by you, he can't completely forget. He's haunted by it. I'd bet my life on it."

Cage loved me. He thought I was perfect. He was the brother every girl deserves. I turned my head and kissed his chest.

"Thank you. I know you really believe that. And I love you for it. But you're wrong."

"Haven't you figured out by now that I'm never wrong?"

Laughing, I reached for another handful of popcorn. I was safe here in this moment. I didn't want to think about anything else.

Chapter Twenty-Two

MARCUS

"He's our father, Marcus. That isn't ever going to change," Amanda said heatedly as she paced in front of the desk, where I'd been trying to pick the summer courses I needed to take. "Besides, I keep seeing that little face and those blond curls and knowing she's our sister. She's a baby who did nothing wrong. She was born. It's not her fault. I want to know her, Marcus. I want to have my dad back in my life again. I hate this. Mom wants us to go see him. Them. She thinks it'll be good for us. Especially you."

Groaning, I leaned back in my chair and stared up at my very determined sister. What had happened to mad Amanda? The one who hated our father and never wanted to see him again? I liked that Amanda. I wanted her back. We felt the same way. Except, of course, the part about Larissa. Every time I thought about her my chest ached. All that time I'd been so fascinated with her little blond curls and happy little claps and squeals, and she'd been my sister. Had that been Willow's plan? She'd thought that by bringing Larissa into my life under false pretenses I'd love her and accept what my father had done? God, how had I been so blind!? Those damn dimples. I was lost the moment she'd flashed them at me. She appeared so wounded and innocent, and the whole freaking time she'd known exactly what her sister was doing to my mama. What Willow had done was unforgivable. She'd lied to me. To my family. And dammit, I was still in love with her.

"They're going to be at the condo this week. He's invited us, and I'm going. I want you there with me. I need you there, Marcus. Please," Amanda begged. "Dad said Tawny wouldn't be there. It'll just be him and Larissa," she assured me then kissed me on the head.

Dinner with Dad, the other woman, and the other kid. Not my idea of a good time. An image of Larissa smiling up at me and demanding I play with her tugged at me.

"Okay, I'll go. But only because you want me to so badly. Not because I want to make amends with him. If you want to, then fine. But it'll never happen for me."

Amanda frowned, then nodded and walked around the table and kissed me on the head.

"Thank you. I really wish you'd get past all this anger and let it go. Then maybe you can see the big picture that everyone else sees. You're living in a tunnel, and if you stay blind for too long you'll miss it."

What the crap did that mean? I stared up at her, and she smirked, then walked out of the room. I guess she thought that was supposed to be deep and meaningful. It was probably the lyrics from some godawful boy band song.

"Amanda," my dad said warmly, and pulled Amanda into his arms. He patted her head, kissed her temple, and whispered something to her. She nodded, he raised his eyes to meet mine. "Marcus. I'm glad you came." I wasn't. But obviously Amanda needed this. I nodded and followed her inside.

"*Martus!*" A loud squeal startled me, and I looked down to see Larissa running toward me with her arms up in the air, grinning. Two little teeth flashed at me. I picked her up, and she smelled just like I remembered.

"How's my princess? I see you got two teeth."

She pointed at her new teeth. "Two teef," she agreed, and placed a wet kiss on my mouth. "Martus, come pay." She'd added a few new words to her vocabulary. I set her down and held her hand.

"You lead the way," I told her, and she pulled me along behind her toward the living room, where toys of all kinds were scattered around the floor. I quickly scanned the room, and Tawny was nowhere to be found. Letting out a sigh of relief, I sat down where Larissa demanded. She pulled a bucket of bright-pink blocks toward me.

"Pinses bocks," she explained, pointing to the picture of Cinderella on one of the blocks.

"My favorite kind," I assured her, and she giggled happily, waiting for me to build her a tower of blocks to knock down.

"She's mentioned you several times," my father said as he walked into the room. I didn't look up at him. Nor did I respond. I came here for two reasons. My sisters, both of them.

Amanda sank down onto the floor on the other side of Larissa.

"Larissa, this is Manda," I said as she studied Amanda.

"Mana," she repeated.

Amanda beamed at her and nodded. "Yes, and it's very nice to meet you, Larissa. Can I play too?"

Larissa grinned brightly. Amanda had said her favorite word.

"Mana pay too." She pushed some blocks toward Amanda.

Amanda eagerly started stacking them. Larissa had that effect on people. She was hard to resist. Much like her aunt. *Aw, damn.*

Larissa was studying me, and I watched as her small smile faded and she looked back at Dad, then at me.

"I 'ont my Lowlow," she whispered as tears filled her eyes. Dad immediately walked over and picked her up.

"Hey, don't cry, sweetheart. You have Marcus here to play with you and Amanda. Remember, I told you Lowlow would be coming tomorrow to see you. Okay?" His voice was so gentle. Had he talked to us like that once? It was hard to see my dad as being softhearted and loving. Larissa sniffed and nodded.

"Down," Larissa demanded, and Dad put her back where she'd been sitting. She smiled tearily up at me. "Lowlow come too."

My chest hurt so badly I was having trouble breathing. Would it ever get easier seeing Larissa? Would memories of Willow always haunt me and rip me apart all over again?

I cleared my throat and nodded.

"Can you show me your other toys?" Amanda asked. She knew I was having a hard time, and she was trying to distract Larissa from any more comments about her beloved aunt. Larissa stood up, nodding, and held out her hand to Amanda. "Come see."

Amanda happily followed the little chubby blonde out of the room. It was like Amanda finally had a real baby doll to play with. She'd always wanted a little sister. Guess she finally got one.

I was alone with my father. Shit.

"You have any plans for the summer?" he asked picking a very neutral topic.

"Online courses," I replied, standing up and walking over to the large windows overlooking the gulf.

"You trying to hurry up and finish?"

"No. I'm making up for lost time." He didn't deserve any more of an explanation. He'd opted out of my life. Turning around before he could say any more I asked, "Where's the new mom?"

"I asked her to let me do this alone."

"Why? Afraid I'll hurt her feelings?"

My father shook his head. "No, I just didn't want her here while I visited with my kids."

"I'm only here for Amanda."

"And Larissa. I'm not a fool, son. I see the way you look at her. You may not want to care about her, but you do."

No reason to lie. "I cared about Larissa before I knew. She's a baby. None of this is her fault."

"And she's your sister."

"And she's my sister," I agreed. No point in arguing. It was the truth.

"Have you spoken to Willow since . . . ?" He didn't finish. He didn't need to.

"No."

He didn't have a response for that. I started to go find the girls, and then his voice stopped me. "She didn't know."

I froze.

"She was devastated. She'd just figured it out. She was there, at the house, having a complete emotional breakdown when you walked in."

I swallowed hard. Did I want to hear this?

"She stripped me bare by listing every person I'd hurt with my actions. She pointed out every sin I'd committed, and she praised the one person who'd been left to pick up the pieces. She praised him rather passionately. How he'd been the one to hold the family I'd betrayed together. She also told me how much she loved him and how my actions and her sister's actions were going to be the reason she lost him."

I grabbed hold of the chair beside me. My knees went weak. The ache from hearing Larissa ask for Willow was nothing compared to the pain searing through my chest now. The things I'd said. Oh, God, *no*.

"She's been left her whole life. She's a good girl. Larissa adores her. While her sister lacks many honorable traits, Willow seems to have them in abundance."

I'd left her.

Just like she'd feared.

The memory of her face when she'd walked into the bedroom that day before my sister had called. She'd looked completely broken, devastated, lost. She'd just found out. She'd come to tell me. And I'd had to leave.

She hadn't known all along.

"What's wrong?" Amanda asked as she walked into the room.

I lifted my head and looked at her. "She didn't know," I whispered, horrified as the words that I'd yelled at her that night as she pleaded with me to stop echoed in my head.

"I never thought she did," Amanda replied. The sadness in her voice was unmistakable. "I tried to tell you that I was pretty sure she was innocent, but you wouldn't listen to me. I wasn't allowed to even speak her name. Every time I tried to talk to you about Willow, you ended up so stupid drunk you couldn't walk."

She knew as well as I did that I'd lost Low, and that it was all my fault.

WILLOW

Dinner with Tawny and Jefferson hadn't been too bad. Larissa had latched on to me and hadn't let go. I'd even tucked her in and read to her until she fell asleep. I knew there was no way I could handle hearing her cry for me when I left. The way she'd clung to me reminded me of how I felt. Afraid I'd lose someone I loved. I wasn't going to stay away any longer. I'd discussed with Tawny meeting her halfway to Mobile and getting Larissa one night a week. That way I could spend time with just her and not have to face that house again. Surprisingly, Jefferson was behind the idea one hundred percent. He apparently didn't like Larissa crying for me either. I wanted to hate him, but when I watched him with Larissa it made it hard. Things happen in life, and you can't control them. It sucks and you have to move on. Holding a grudge against Tawny and Jefferson was pointless. It only hurt Larissa, and she was innocent.

Cage's bedroom door opened, and he walked out frowning. "Are you sure you're okay with this? I'd feel better about going if you'd come too."

I shook my head. I wasn't going to be his shadow anymore. He needed to get back to his life. Tonight I wanted him to go out and have a good time with his friends. I was fine right here.

"I have chocolate ice cream and two seasons' worth of *True Blood*. So go. Me and vampire Eric will be just fine. I promise."

He sighed and reached over and hugged me. "Okay, fine. I'm going. But you call me the minute you feel an anxiety attack, or just if you get upset or—"

"Cage, *go* now." I pointed toward the door.

"I'm going. But I've got my phone with me."

"I heard you, Cage. Go."

Once the door closed behind him, I got out my chocolate ice cream and headed for the couch. Tonight I would forget about everything except hot Viking vampires.

Chapter Twenty-Three

MARCUS

"Don't look now, but Cage is headed this way," Dewayne muttered, jerking me back to the present. I'd gotten lost in my thoughts. Since Dad had informed me of how incredibly wrong I'd been about Willow, I'd done nothing but replay every awful word I'd said to her. I searched the crowd until I found Cage walking our way. He was alone.

"Sorry man, I didn't know he was going to be here tonight or I'd have given you a heads up," Preston whispered from across the table.

"Stop babying him. He's gonna have to deal with it eventually," Rock said with an unapologetic shrug. He was right, of course.

"Didn't expect you out tonight," Preston said as Cage came to a stop at the table.

"I needed a night out. Low insisted I go do something."

"She didn't come out with you?" I surprised everyone, including myself, by asking.

Cage frowned at me, then tilted his head as if he was studying me. I stared at him, waiting on an answer while he decided if I deserved one or not.

"No. She had a bad experience the last time I talked her into getting out of the apartment and coming here with me," he replied slowly and evenly. The night I'd grabbed the girl and danced with her. Damn, the list of marks against me was endless.

"Uh, well, it's good you got out tonight. You don't do that much anymore," Preston piped up in an attempt to break the tension.

Cage continued to glare at me. "I've had other priorities."

I wanted to hate him. Because he'd been there for her. Because he'd been what I hadn't. But I couldn't hate him. Instead, I was grateful someone had taken care of her.

"Is she okay?" I needed to know. Anything. Just something. I needed something.

Cage let out a hard laugh and shook his head like he couldn't believe what he was hearing. "No, Marcus she isn't. But one day she will be. It isn't like she hasn't been left before. She'll survive."

If he'd intended to slice me open, he'd succeeded. I needed air. Standing up, I grabbed my water and turned around to leave.

"If it were me you'd fucked over, you'd be dead to me. But it wasn't me. It was Low. And she isn't like most people. If you've managed to put away enough of that sheltered little rich boy righteous fury and figured out what an enormous mistake you made, then it isn't too late. Yet." Then Cage York turned and walked away. Through the crowd and out the front door. I stood there replaying his words in my head. Then I broke into a run.

Cage's Mustang wasn't parked outside. I stood looking up at the window of the apartment, and although the lights were off, I could see the glow from the television. She was here. Just like Cage had said. I took the stairs two at a time and halted at the door. I no longer had a key. She'd have to come to the door. And she might slam it in my face. I rubbed my palms across the tops of my jeans and took a few deep breaths. Did I even deserve this? If there was any chance she'd forgive me, was I even worthy of her forgiveness? No. I wasn't. But I was selfish. I wanted Low. That's all I cared about. Raising my hand, I rapped on the door, then waited while my heart tried to pound out of my chest. The deadbolt unlatched and the knob turned. Waiting, I stood praying she'd listen.

WILLOW

"Marcus?" Had I fallen asleep on the couch? Was this a dream? It wouldn't be the first dream I'd had of Marcus over the past couple of months. I blinked several times and stared. It sure felt real.

"Low," he whispered almost reverently. This had to be a dream. This was my dream Marcus. The one who didn't hate me. The one who still loved me. I turned from the door, not wanting to dream anymore. It hurt too much. I was tired of hurting.

"Low, please, just listen to me, please," Marcus pleaded from behind me. Turning around, I saw that he had stepped inside.

"Am I asleep?" I asked him, confused. Because this dream was way too real.

"No" came his simple reply. I watched as he closed the door behind him.

"Why're you here?"

He took another step closer, and I took one back. Sookie screamed on the television and I jumped, startled. Reaching for the remote, I pressed mute and then looked back up at Marcus.

"I wanted to talk to you. I don't deserve for you to listen to me, but I'm willing to beg if it'll do any good."

Frowning, I sat down on the couch and pulled my legs underneath me.

"I'm listening," I replied, and he visibly relaxed.

"I'm sorry," he started, and closed his eyes tightly, taking a deep breath before opening them and gazing at me with so many emotions. "That day. You came here to tell me. You'd just found out. But I didn't know that. I knew you were upset, but then my sister called, and my mother had taken a bottle full of prescription painkillers."

I knew this already, but I let him continue.

"We almost lost her. But they pumped her stomach and I stood there with my sister waiting for her to come back to us. When she woke up, she said Dad had brought her the divorce papers and he was moving in with another woman. She'd tried to kill herself. I went to the dealership and demanded someone give me his new address. I was going to beat him to a bloody pulp for what he'd done to my mother. What he'd driven her to. The fear that had gripped me all afternoon as I watched my mother's life hang in the balance transferred to fury. Then when I walked in and saw you and your sister, I couldn't think straight, Low. I felt betrayed. Not by my dad, but by you. You being there at that house, I didn't see how there was any way you could not know. I was positive you knew. I didn't trust you. I didn't listen to you. I just turned all that fear and fury on you and lashed out at you. And so help me God, I'll regret it for the rest of my life."

Tears clung to my eyelashes as I watched the turmoil and regret in Marcus's face as he replayed the day he'd shattered me. My heart ached for him. I sniffed and reached up to wipe the tears away.

"I forgive you." I did. It didn't change much, but I did forgive him. I took a deep breath and realized it was easier to breathe.

Knowing he didn't believe I'd betrayed him took the heaviness away. Most of it, at least.

Marcus stared at me. I'd surprised him. He hadn't expected me to forgive him.

"You forgive me?" he asked hoarsely.

"Yes, I do. I understand what happened. The entire situation was a nightmare. But life sucks, and you get over it and move on."

He swallowed so hard I could see his throat constrict.

"I love you, Low."

I wanted to believe that, and maybe he did. But I couldn't survive him again. I'd reached my limit of heartbreak.

"Marcus, what we had, it was . . . it was incredible. It was amazing. I've never had anything like that before. I'll cherish it for the rest of my life."

"Don't, Low. Please," Marcus choked out.

I forced a smile through my tears. They were flowing freely now. This was our closure.

"I can't do that again. Once was all I can handle. I never thought I'd open up like that to anyone. To be free and trusting. But I did. And I don't regret it. I never will. But I've met my quota of abandonment in my life. I need to protect *me*."

Marcus let out a long rattled breath. I watched as he ran his hands through his hair. He was beautiful. And he had once been mine. I was thankful for that.

"Low, I will love you until the day I die," he declared, staring down at me with moisture glistening in his eyes. I'd love him, too. But it wasn't enough.

"I'm sorry," I whispered.

We stared at each other as the heaviness of where we'd ended up settled on us.

He took another deep breath then he nodded. "I can't force you to trust me. I deserve this." His voice was shaky.

"You deserve to be happy," I assured him. Because he did.

"I'll never be happy without you," he replied. The anguish in his eyes was so hard to ignore.

"Yes, you will."

"Low, God, I'm so sorry. Please, just can I prove to you that I'm not going anywhere? I'll spend the rest of my life proving to you I'll never hurt you again."

The conversation we'd had on the floor of his bathroom not too long ago came back to me. It was so similar. He'd been so sure he'd never hurt me again. He'd always be there. Marcus had been too sheltered. He didn't handle bad things well. I needed someone who wouldn't leave me when the bad things came.

"I can't. I tried. It didn't work. I can't keep expecting Cage to pick up the pieces when my life falls apart. It's time I learned to fix my own problems. Deal with bad stuff on my own. And that means I can't trust my heart with anyone. Because I'm weak there."

Marcus took two long strides and knelt down on the floor in front of me. I could smell him. So good. So clean. My Marcus.

"Low, I swear you can trust me. Please. I miss you. I ache for you. I need you, Low. Please, baby, please."

A sob rattled my chest and I shook my head. "I can't."

He dropped his head to my knees, and we sat there while silent tears fell. I reached out and touched his hair. Remembering the feel of him. I relished in the smell of him as it surrounded me. Finally he raised his head slowly and looked at me one last time before standing and walking away. When the door closed behind him, I curled up on the couch and cried until I didn't have any more tears to cry.

Chapter Twenty-Four

MARCUS

I'd seen glimpses of Willow at the bar. She never came in for long. Normally, it was because she was at work and needed something from the supply room. She always smiled. It was friendly. That was it. Looking for her had become my only pastime. I was beginning to wonder if I was becoming a stalker. The only thing that kept me sane was she wasn't with another guy. She was rarely with Cage. She lived with him, but he wasn't there often, I'd heard. He was making up for lost time, apparently.

I glanced around the restaurant nervously, looking for Low. I needed to get a seat in her section before she came walking out into the dining room. Otherwise, there was a good chance she'd have the hostess seat me somewhere else. I followed the short brunette back to a booth she assured me was one of Willow's tonight.

"Low should be with you in just a moment." The girl's high-pitched voice startled me.

I nodded. "Thanks." I quickly took a seat, placing the small package I had brought in with me on the seat and out of view. I didn't want her to have a chance to refuse it. I intended to leave it on the table when I left. That way, if she was determined to reject my gift, she'd have to come find me first.

She stepped around the corner, looking down at the small pad in her hand. A pencil was stuck behind her ear, and her hair was pulled up into a messy bun on the back of her head. I missed her so much. I watched as she lifted her head. Those large expressive green eyes that haunted my dreams locked on me, and she stumbled. The urge to jump up and go touch her was unbearable. I forced myself to remain in my seat, but my eyes ate her up as she composed herself and continued over to my booth.

"Marcus," she said, smiling nervously.

"Hello, Low," I replied. The sweet honeysuckle scent that clung to her filled the small booth.

"Are you, uh, waiting on someone?"

I shook my head and grinned. "Nope. Just me."

The relief on her face gave me hope.

"Oh, okay. In that case, what can I get you to drink?"

"I'd like some sweet tea, please."

Willow reached for the pencil tucked behind her ear and

quickly jotted it down. I'd never seen her write down drink orders before. Could my presence have her that rattled that she needed to write down "sweet tea"? God, I hoped so.

"Okay, I'll be right back." She flashed me a smile that didn't reach her eyes, then quickly spun around and headed directly for the kitchen. She didn't stop at any of her other tables to check on them. Willow needed a moment. Because of me. For the first time in weeks I was able to take a deep breath. Just maybe I could reach her again. Those damn thick walls she'd erected around her heart terrified me.

WILLOW

I can do this. I can do this. I CAN do this.

"You okay, Low?" Seth asked, stopping beside me with a tray of drinks.

"Um, yeah, I'm good. Just needed a breather." I forced yet another smile and reached for the sweet tea I'd fixed for Marcus.

Seth nodded and headed back out the door into the dining room. I needed to do the same. I ran my hand over my hair and smoothed my apron down, then rolled my eyes at my ridiculous behavior. This was Marcus. He'd shattered my heart. I did not care what he thought of me. My appearance was of no consequence.

I headed back out into the dining room and stopped at my other tables to check on them. I needed to get another bottle of tartar sauce, a glass of water, and some lemons. And I still had Marcus's drink in my hands. I had to get this over with.

He was leaning back in the booth, watching me as I approached. I'd felt his gaze on me while I'd checked on the other customers. It was a miracle I hadn't tripped and fallen from my nervous reaction to his attention.

"Here ya go." I placed the tea on the table in front of him. "You ready to order?"

"The blackened grouper sounds good," he replied.

I wanted to curl up in his lap. How ridiculous was that? Just hearing him talk had me needing to touch him and feel his arms around me again. *Ugh!*

"Do you not recommend that?"

I snapped out of my internal obsessing and looked at him. "Huh?"

Marcus grinned at me, and my insides went all crazy. "You're frowning. I was wondering if I'd ordered the wrong thing?"

My face instantly warmed, and I shook my head, staring down at my order pad in an attempt to hide my blushing. "Oh, no. That's really good. The grouper is nice and fresh."

"Do you suggest I try those sweet potato fries?"

"Well, they're different. Um, maybe you should stick with the regular fries."

Marcus nodded and handed me the menu. "Regular fries it is, then."

I reached to take his menu and fought the urge to look at him. I knew he was watching me. If I lifted my head, our eyes would meet. I wasn't that strong yet. Maybe one day I would be. But I needed time. Slipping the menu under my arm, I hurried back to the kitchen. I needed another breather.

After handing Marcus his check, I'd once again scurried back to the safety of the kitchen. I slumped against the back wall behind the industrial-sized dishwasher and let out a frustrated groan. This had been torture. Marcus had been friendly and talkative. He'd watched my every move as if I were the most fascinating thing he'd ever seen. I was a ball of nerves. Twice, girls I didn't know who obviously knew him had come up to him and done everything they could to coax him to go out dancing with them. He'd brushed them off. Harshly. I'd loved it. Each time I'd lost the battle and glanced over at his booth, his eyes had been locked on me. Even when he'd had uninvited guests, his gaze never seemed to waiver.

"Low, your friend left a tip on the table, and a box with your name written rather impressively for a guy."

Unable to mask my curiosity, I rushed back to the booth where Marcus had been seated. He'd left a fifty-dollar bill to pay for his twenty-dollar meal. Frowning, I pocketed the money and picked up the package he'd left. I ran my finger over my name. I recognized his neat handwriting.

"Hey, Seth, I'll be right back," I called out as I headed for the back door. I needed privacy. Once I was outside safely hidden out of the way, I opened it.

It was a 2006 Guns N' Roses Chinese Democracy T-shirt, signed by all the members of the band. A small note was tucked inside it, and I caught it just before it fell onto the muddy gravel.

Willow,

There's a story behind this shirt. I actually went to this concert opening night in Miami. It has been one of my prized possessions ever since. It's special because it was the only thing my dad ever took me to. He knew how badly I wanted to go. I'd just turned fifteen, and he came to my room one night with two tickets. They weren't just any tickets. They were backstage passes. He'd used every connection he could to get his hands on those tickets. It's the only fond memory I have of my dad. Maybe that's why it was so special.

Anyway, I want you to have it. I'd like to see it on you instead of stuck back in a drawer in my dresser. It's one of the good parts of me, and I'd like to know it's in your hands.

I love you. I always will.
Marcus

Chapter Twenty-Five

MARCUS

Larissa kicked happily in the pool as she bobbed in the shallow end with a life jacket on. Dad had called to let me know they were at the condo for the week and Larissa would like to see me. I wanted to see her, too. He and Tawny had gone out shopping and left me alone with Larissa, since I still didn't care to see Larissa's mother. I didn't like Tawny. I never would. She hadn't just been the cause of my mother's and sister's pain, but she'd mistreated Low all her life. For that reason alone, I'd disliked her before I'd known her.

"My Lowlow," Larissa squealed, slapping at the water. I followed her worshipful gaze to see Willow walking out of the house in a royal-blue bikini. Whoa.

"Hello, sweet girl. I've missed you, too," Willow replied,

grinning down at Larissa as she continued to squeal and slap at the water. Willow glanced shyly over at me, and I was pretty sure I'd swallowed my tongue.

"Hello, Marcus."

"Low," I managed to reply.

"I hope you don't mind. Tawny called and said Larissa had woken up asking for me, and that you had her at the pool today if I wanted to come swim with her a little."

She was here.

She was talking to me.

She was in a bikini.

"Uh, no, I don't mind at all."

There was nothing in her hands. She wasn't brining back the shirt I'd left her three nights ago. She was keeping it. I couldn't help but smile.

"My Lowlow," Larissa squealed as Low lowered herself into the water and made her way over to her.

"Look at you, swimming all around like a big girl," Low cooed at her. Larissa ate it up and started spinning in circles, anxious to show off her new trick.

"Wow! And you can do tricks."

"Martus ticks." Larissa pointed a little finger at me.

"I'll bet Marcus can do tricks," Willow agreed. I wanted to show her just how many tricks I could do. Especially with her in that bikini.

A Frisbee zoomed close to Willow's head, and before I could open my mouth to warn her, she had grabbed it.

"Hey, nice catch." A guy with a buzz cut and way more muscles than was normal jogged up, grinning at Willow like he'd just hit the jackpot.

"Yes, well, be careful next time. You could've hit her in the head," Willow chided him politely, nodding toward Larissa.

"Oh, yeah, sorry about that. The wind caught it. I'll just move out farther."

Willow shot him that heart-stopping smile of hers and he looked a little shaken. I completely understood how he felt. But he needed to walk away. Now.

"Martus ticks," Larissa demanded.

Willow cut her eyes to me, smirking. "I do believe you're going to have to show us your tricks. The queen has spoken."

Standing up, I walked over to the diving board. I jumped up on it. I felt like a teenager again. I was excited about showing off in front of a girl. Willow's appreciative gaze was traveling down my body. Well, damn. Now I couldn't concentrate, and I was going to get a boner, which would be obvious in these swim trunks. I needed to hurry up. I ran out and did a backflip and dove into the water.

When my head broke through the top of the water, both Willow and Larissa were clapping.

"Bravo. I'm impressed. I wasn't aware country club boys

knew any tricks," Willow teased. She started to swim toward the ladder but stopped beside me.

"Thanks for the shirt. I love it," she said in a soft whisper, then darted off for the ladder. She loved my shirt. She wasn't going to give back my gift. My heart sped up at the thought of her wearing it.

I watched in fascination as she climbed out of the pool. Her bikini bottom was hugging her butt like a second skin. The water running down her body glistened as the sun hit it. When she turned around to give me a front view, I was really glad to be underwater.

"Let's see if I can't one-up that. I didn't grow up jumping off diving boards. I grew up jumping off bridge pilings into the gulf." She winked. She actually winked. Was Willow flirting with me? Her hips swayed as she walked, and I forgot everything but her almost naked body.

"Lowlow ticks," Larissa declared.

"Yep, Low is gonna do some tricks," I murmured, unable to think coherently. Shit. She was going to bounce. All my schoolboy fantasies came rushing back, and I wondered if drool was trickling out of my mouth. She ran and jumped into a toe touch, then tucked her legs, flipped backward, and broke the water with a perfect dive.

Dear God, that image was going to come in handy later. Tonight. In my shower.

Larissa was cheering as Willow swam back to us. I managed to shake myself out of my lustful thoughts and clapped.

"I don't think I can beat that. But by all means you go right ahead and show us some more tricks." I shot her a wicked grin and she blushed.

I closed the distance between us and leaned down until my lips were inches from her ear.

"I love you," I whispered, and then, without looking to see her reaction, I swam away. I needed some distance. Because I was real close to grabbing her and kissing her until I was at least minimally sated. Which might be impossible.

WILLOW

"I love you"

Those three words Marcus had whispered in my ear repeated themselves all evening. Long after I'd kissed Larissa good-bye and left Marcus with a wave. Would it ever get easy? We would always be in each other's lives. I wanted to prove we could be around each other and Larissa and have it not be awkward. All I'd proved was that I wasn't over Marcus Hardy. Not by a long shot.

"What's up with the frown?" Cage asked, walking into the kitchen and jumping up to take a seat on the bar right beside where I was chopping vegetables for my salad.

"Just thinking. Move your butt over." I nudged his leg with the back of my hand.

"Talked to Marcus lately?"

What kind of question was that? "Yes."

"When?"

"Today."

"He make you frown?"

"No. He was nice. We were nice."

"Nice, huh? So, you thinking about that not-trusting-him thing? Decided yet if you might could take one more chance?"

I put the knife down and looked up at him. "Cage, what's this about?"

Cage rubbed his chin thoughtfully. "I think you're making a mistake."

Me too. "Why?"

"Marcus did leave you. *But* he came back. He wanted to come back. Everyone else who left you didn't want to come back, Low. They left because they wanted to. Marcus didn't want to leave. It completely tore him up."

I gripped the edge of the counter with both hands. He'd come back. "He did," I whispered.

Cage reached down and squeezed my shoulder.

"Yeah, he did."

"Do you think he'll leave me again?"

Cage let out a long, heavy sigh. "Well, things happen in life, Low. Hell, I could die tomorrow, and then I'll have left you. We can't control the future. But I can promise you that Marcus

Hardy loves you more than anyone else is ever going to love you. Other than me, of course."

I chuckled. "Of course."

"Nobody loves you like I love ya, baby," he teased. Jumping back down off the counter, he pulled me into a hug. "Take a chance, Low."

"What do I do? I told him no," I mumbled into Cage's shoulder.

"I've seen the guy, Low. Walk up to him and say you love him. You changed your mind. You want to give it another go. I can promise you he won't argue with you."

I leaned back and stared up at Cage. "You think?"

"I know."

"Okay. I guess I'll text him to meet me somewhere."

"That sounds like a really good idea."

Cage started to turn around and walk away, but I reached out and grabbed his arm to stop him. "Cage?"

He let me pull him back with his trademark wicked grin firmly in place. "Yes?"

"Why're you doing this?"

"Doing what?"

I put one hand on my hip and cocked an eyebrow. He knew good and well what I was talking about.

"Why're you all for me talking to Marcus, giving him another chance? Weren't you planning on marrying me eventually? I'd think this screws up your ten-year plan."

Cage chuckled and draped an arm over my shoulders. "I guess it does kinda mess up my well-thought-out future, but the thing is, Marcus makes you happy. He can love you in ways I can't. I'm all kinds of fucked up, Low. You and I both know I'd never make a good husband." He grimaced at the word and I couldn't help but giggle.

"Oh, I'm well aware you'd make a horrible husband, but I'm just a little surprised you think someone else is good enough for me."

"I never said Marcus was good enough for you. Don't go getting all carried away. All I said was he makes you happy, and I think if anyone could love you as much as I do, it'd be Marcus. He's so lovesick when it comes to you, baby, it's kinda pathetic to watch."

I hoped he was right.

Chapter Twenty-Six

MARCUS

I want to talk to you. Could you come over to the apartment?

I stared at the text from Willow. Standing outside the apartment door again, I had a horrible case of déjà vu. Last time I'd come here, she'd completely dashed every dream I'd ever had. Now I was back. I raised my hand to knock, and I froze. Did I want to do this? Could I take much more of this? If she had decided we didn't need to be around each other at all until I learned to control my need to profess my love for her, I might go jump off a damn bridge. No. She wouldn't do that. I was being as dramatic as a damn girl. My knuckles hit the smooth wood and it was done. I was here.

The door opened almost immediately, and Willow stood there smiling nervously.

"You came," she said. I could hear the relief in her voice. Had she really thought I'd turn her down?

"You ask. I come."

She chewed on her bottom lip, and I looked away. I couldn't think about her lips.

"Come in. Do you want a drink?"

She was wringing her hands and biting her lip. Willow was nervous.

"No. I'm good."

I wanted to get on with this. Our combined nervous energy was driving me crazy. I wanted to grab her and reassure her. But I couldn't. Not anymore.

"Oh." She looked around and then back at me. "Okay, well, then would you mind sitting down?"

This was getting more fascinating by the second. I walked over and sank down onto the worn couch, where so many of my favorite moments with Willow had taken place.

"You gonna sit?" I asked as she paced a few times and shot nervous glances my way.

"Uh, no, don't think I can."

Okay.

"Low, what's this about?"

She stopped and stood directly in front of me with the coffee table between us.

"I love you."

My heart almost stopped beating in my chest. She hadn't spoken those words since the last time I'd held her in my arms.

"And you did leave me. But . . . but you came back. No one's ever come back. They leave me and that's it. They want to leave me. You didn't. And you came back."

I wanted to stand up and reach across the table and jerk her into my arms, but I wasn't sure I could stand up just yet. I needed to hear everything she had to say. "Yes, I came back. My heart never left you."

"I miss you."

This time I stood up and walked around the table. "I miss you. Every second of every day," I whispered. Her eyes followed me until I was inches from her.

"I trust you."

I needed more than that.

"You trust me," I repeated.

She nodded, and her hand came up and caressed the side of my arm.

"I want to try again."

Those were the words I needed to hear.

WILLOW

His mouth was on mine before I could respond. I gasped in surprise, and his tongue took advantage of it and tangled with mine., tasting everywhere. I gripped the hair on the back of his head as he pulled me up hard against him. Then we were on the couch. His mouth left mine, and he began raining kisses all over my face and down my neck. He told me how much he loved me over and over again as he ran his hands down my back, cupping my butt and tucking me up against him.

Moaning into his mouth, I nibbled and tasted every smooth inch of it. I felt my shirt begin to lift as Marcus's fingers brushed against my skin.

"Lift your arms." His demand was needy. I didn't argue. I lifted my arms, and my shirt was ripped off my body, and then Marcus's hands were back on my face, and he was kissing me. His hands slowly traveled down my neck and traced my collarbone. I moaned in frustration. Then his hands covered my bra. The front clasp came undone, and my bra fell away, slipping down my arms. Marcus stopped kissing me and sat back while he slowly pulled the bra off my wrists and tossed it aside.

"I love you," he breathed, lifting his gaze from my naked breasts to my eyes.

"I love you, too," I replied breathlessly.

"I want you, Low."

I nodded because I couldn't form words.

Pulling me up against him, he kissed me, and I fumbled with the hem of his shirt.

"Off," I whispered against his mouth. In one swift movement he jerked it off. I pressed against him, sighing at the feel of his warm skin naked against mine.

"Low," he groaned in my ear as he trailed kisses down my neck.

I stopped breathing, watching as he stopped kissing at the top of my chest. His warm breath tickled my nipples, making them even harder.

When he finally pulled one into his mouth, I cried out his name and let myself go. I was ready to trust Marcus. Completely.

"I want inside you," he whispered in my ear while his hand slipped under my skirt and inside my panties. He gently ran a finger against me, and his body shuddered as I made a whimpering sound.

"You are so wet. So perfect. Everything I've always wanted. Please, baby, please let me love you."

I pulled away from his embrace and stood up. The panic on his face made me smile. I slipped off my skirt and panties, then crawled back into his lap.

"Holy shit, you're gorgeous," he whispered as he ran his hands down my chest in a caress. He treated me as if I were some kind of priceless piece of art as he worshipped me with his hands. I was ready to start begging him to slip a hand between my legs again when he picked me up and laid me back on the couch.

"I love touching you and looking at your body. But I need to get closer," he explained as he unzipped his pants and slid them off along with his underwear. I wanted to touch him.

Leaning up on my elbows, I reached out. He grabbed my hand before I could feel him and chuckled. "Not such a good idea. I want inside you before I explode."

He grabbed his jeans and pulled a condom out of his wallet.

"Can I put it on you?"

He shook his head. "Again, not a good idea. Not this time. I need you too much right now. I may embarrass myself."

Smiling, I leaned back as he covered my body. His knee pushed my legs open as he sank down between them.

"Oh my God!" I cried out as his erection touched me. I'd never felt him with no layers between us. I couldn't stop myself from bucking, trying to get closer.

"Holy hell, this is gonna kill me," Marcus breathed. "I want to fill you up so damn bad, but I have to go easy. It'll hurt you if I don't."

"Please, Marcus. Stop making me wait. I need you. I want you inside me. Completing me."

Marcus's mouth claimed mine, and his tongue thrust into my mouth as his erection pressed into my opening. I was ready for him. I could feel by the easy way he started to slide inside. I lifted my hips, and he reached down and pressed them back against the couch stopping me from making this go faster.

He slowly eased into me. "So tight. It's so tight, Low. So incredibly hot and tight," he whispered against my mouth. "I love you. I want you to know that I love you. I will always love you."

I started to assure him that I loved him, too, when a sharp pain startled me as he sank all the way inside me and stilled. I held on to his arms tightly until the burning eased away.

"I'm okay," I assured him as he kissed my face and ran his hands through my hair like he was trying to soothe me. "Please, I want more," I begged.

Marcus hissed through his teeth as he pulled back, and then moved back in. A tingling started growing inside me as his arms began trembling at my sides.

"I never knew it could feel like this," he said with a low moan.

"I want it faster. Can you do it faster?" I asked, squeezing his biceps as the sensation in my body began to build.

"Oh yeah, I can go faster," he assured me as he began pumping into me at a steadier pace. It was exactly what I was craving.

Just as my body exploded into mindless pleasure, I heard Marcus cry out my name as his whole body jerked and shuttered over me.

When I opened my eyes, I was staring at the smooth defined pecs on Marcus's chest. I inhaled him. I was wrapped in his arms, and our legs were tangled together. Which I thought was rather delicious. I wasn't sure how much clothing I had on, or if I had any. I was definitely topless. That much I could tell.

I buried my face in his chest to muffle my giggle.

"What's so funny?" Marcus's sleepy voice asked, amused.

"I'm naked," I said against his chest.

His chest vibrated from his chuckle.

"Yes, and it's incredible," he replied.

He reached down and pulled the quilt up over us.

"I can't believe we both managed to sleep on this couch," I whispered, wondering if Cage had come home and seen us like this.

"I need to talk to Cage about buying this couch. It now holds some pretty intense memories for me. I want it."

Unable to hold back my grin, I tilted my head back and stared up at him. I loved his sleep-mussed hair.

"How do you feel?" he asked, studying me carefully.

"Wonderful," I replied honestly.

A sexy smirk touched his lips. "Me too."

His warm hand moved down my back and began to caress my hip.

"You're so soft," he murmured. His heavy-lidded eyes made my insides do all kinds of funny things.

"Cage may be here," I reminded him, sliding my leg up between his legs.

"Hmm . . . He is."

My eyes flew open wide.

Marcus chuckled. "Relax, he didn't see anything. I had you all covered up when he walked in."

"What did he say?"

I believe his exact words were "Well, it's about fucking time."

Giggling, I leaned up and kissed his chin. "What did you say?"

Marcus kissed my head. "I agreed wholeheartedly."

Chapter Twenty-Seven

MARCUS

Cheers, clapping, and whistling ensued when I walked into Live Bay two nights later with Low tucked closely to my side.

"Hot damn!"

"Hallelujah!"

"It's about time."

"Finally!"

Willow glanced up at me, smiling. "I guess they're happy about this."

She had no idea.

"Yes, I'm pretty sure nothing short of our marriage would make them happier. They weren't fans of the Willow-less Marcus."

"Oh."

"Yes, 'Oh.'"

Willow kissed my cheek, and our crowd went wild.

"That's what I'm talking about. Lick all over him," Preston hooted as we came up to the table.

"I'd even be okay with some PDA at this point," Dewayne drawled.

"Hello to all of you, too," Willow piped up.

"You have no idea how badly you were missed," Preston said.

Willow glanced up at me. "I have an idea."

"I'm taking my girl to dance and away from all of you. You're making me sound pathetic."

"You were pathetic," Dewayne responded.

I was. No point in arguing.

Pulling Willow into my arms, I enjoyed her soft curves and sweet honeysuckle scent. Nothing in my life had ever felt as right as she did in my arms.

WILLOW

"I can't believe you're moving out." Cage stood in the living room, frowning. "If I'd known you'd leave me I'd never have helped the jackass out and convinced you to give him another chance."

I had my suitcase packed and the key he'd given me in my outstretched hand.

"Don't say that, Cage. I'm not leaving you. I'm releasing you."

"Who the hell said I wanted to be released?"

"I did. You've been my best friend, savior, family, and safe haven for so long. I've always come first in your life. You put your wants and needs on hold to make sure I'm happy. I love you. And it's time I let you go. You're free to just be my friend. You don't have to drop everything to come save me or pick up the pieces. I'm a big girl now. If my world falls apart again, I'll handle it."

Cage reached out and took the key, then grabbed my hand and jerked me into a hug.

"He won't ever leave you, Low. That's the only way I can let you walk out that door. I know he won't. The boy is a goner."

I nodded against his chest. "I don't think he will either."

"And I don't regret anything. I'd do it all again. You know that, right?"

I nodded, feeling my eyes fill up with tears. "You're my family, Cage. You always will be."

"You, too, Low. Always."

Marcus cleared his throat from the doorway. I stepped back and wiped my tears before he could see them.

"Take care of her," Cage told Marcus.

"I will."

Cage nodded and tucked my key into his pocket.

"I guess I'm going on that road trip. I'll have a lot of free time on my hands now."

"Go. Have fun," I said.

Cage grinned. "Okay." He nodded toward the couch. "And just take the couch. I'm not taking your money."

"I want to pay you for it. You're gonna need to replace it."

"I'm thinking of putting a few blow-up mattresses out here. Might have a few orgies."

"*Ugh!* Shut up, Cage." I shoved him making him lose his balance. Chuckling, he shrugged. "Hey, I thought you wanted me to live a little."

"You're crazy, Cage York."

Marcus came up behind me and took my suitcase. "You ready?"

I smiled back at him and nodded.

I was ready. I was ready for everything tomorrow might bring.

ABBI GLINES is the author of *The Vincent Boys* and *The Vincent Brothers* in addition to several other YA novels. A devoted book lover, Abbi lives with her family in Alabama. She maintains a Twitter addiction at @abbiglines and can also be found at AbbiGlines.com.